BORN
FOR THE
GAME

Mike DeLucia

Other Books by Mike DeLucia

Being Brothers
Madness: The Man Who Changed Basketball
Settling a Score
Boycott the Yankees: A Call to Action by a Lifelong Yankees
Fan

Foreword

A blind man knocks himself unconscious by tripping over his dog's bowl and smashing his forehead into a radiator. He is awakened by his dog licking the blood off of his face...When he opens his eyes, he could see!

At least that's what my brother, Joey, told me when we were kids in the 1970s. I believed him because it made complete sense. Firstly, I witnessed people, besides Fonzie, punch broken machines to life again. Secondly, it was common knowledge that humans only use 10% of their brain capacity (another 1970's myth). And most importantly, my brother had sworn to it, after all. While I can't say for certain if the story is the truth or a myth, it is, however, the inspiration for this book.

My belief in the blind man's phenomenon led me on a journey that began with Benny, a prospect signed by the Yankees right out of high school but released a few years later, who spent the next ten years watching TV sports, coaching Little League, and playing softball. The movie began (I always see my books as films) with Benny up at bat in the last inning of a game. The fans cheer as a plump, over-forty pitcher releases an underarm fastball. Benny swings and connects. The centerfielder confidently tracks the ball to the fence, leaps, and catches it in the web of his glove, robbing Benny of the game-winning homerun. After the loss, Benny ponders his final at-bat while sitting in his car at a red light. The camera goes to slow motion as a car slams him from behind and propels his head into the windshield. The scene cuts to Benny waking up in a hospital bed. He sits up, causing alarms to sound, and a clutch of nurses rush to his aid.

"Five Months Later" appears as Benny is cooking dinner at home. A blotchy mark on his forehead is all that remains of his injuries. While he flips a burger, he kicks a cabinet door shut, which causes a jar to fall off the edge of the countertop. The camera goes to slow motion as Benny catches the jar just before it shatters on the floor. Other examples of his heightened dexterity occur before the plot moves back to the softball field displaying a montage of acrobatic catches, base stealing, and 450-foot homeruns—all against the plump, over-forty pitcher who shut him down in the previous game.

These and other such scenes, kept me company on many nights when I had trouble sleeping, or while driving my car, or other times when I just wanted to exist in Benny's world for a short while. These moments were not anything close to a story, they were a collection of scenes. There were times I visited Benny often and other times when I didn't think of him for years, but the story I referred to as The Baseball Movie, morphed inside of my imagination for decades. Benny went from being a man, to a boy, to Ryan Stone, the story's final and most intriguing protagonist. Not only has Benny's character been removed, so has the plot-point of blind man's anomaly. While much of The Baseball Movie has evolved, the concept of being the greatest of all time and the challenges accompanying that lofty goal, remained the crux of the story.

What does it take to be the greatest at anything? This is a universal question and dreaming about it is a universal fantasy. Someone has to be the best. Why not me? Why not you? The possibility of it, albeit slight, exists, and that's what makes it so much fun to imagine.

Although it has taken nearly a lifetime to complete, The Baseball Movie officially became the novel, Born For The Game and was finally released from my imagination in the summer of 2021. Freeing something that's been bouncing around inside for fifty years is an extraordinary feeling, indeed. If I'd gone my whole life without completing it, I'm sure I would have felt deep regret.

The night I finished the first draft of the manuscript, I raised a glass…or three… of Prosecco with my wife Lil and will do the same when I tear open the Amazon envelope, grasp the book in my hand, and flip through its pages.

Salute!

~ **Mike DeLucia**
2021

CHAPTER 1

A speeding red Ferrari weaves recklessly around moving cars on a Los Angeles freeway at dawn. Its driver, Phineas Stone, a handsome dwarf in his late fifties with a goatee and highlighted hair, rocks the stick shift and maneuvers the modified pedals like a brazen NASCAR pro. He sniffs a popper and screams, "Yaaaa, motherfucker!"

Ito Hachi jogs with purpose along a mansion corridor lined with cherry blossom mosaics, canvasses of Asian lettering, floating wall shelves with jade sculptures, and an Ogata Kōrin original of colorful spring flowers. Ito wears a tan, fitted gi with black Adidas martial-arts shoes. He is in his late fifties but presents a decade younger. He is lean, with facial hair, a ponytail, diamond earrings, and neck tattoos.

In hot pursuit of Phineas' Ferrari is a standard-issue black Dodge Charger punching through the vaporous air with a synthesized siren and flashing dash strobe. Its driver is Cole Simmons, a sweaty, pock-faced man in his mid-seventies, who snarls, "I got ya now, ya little son of a bitch!"

A scratchy voice hisses through the dash radio, "Detective Cole, we have spike strips ahead. Desist your pursuit. I repeat,

1

desist your—" Cole smacks off the transmitter. "Screw you, man. I'm cuffing that prick!"

Hovering above Phineas is a police helicopter shooting out flashing lights and bellowing down like an angry droid, "All drivers pull to the right and shut off your engines." It repeats this edict several times then shoots along the morning sky like some tremulous, prehistoric insect.

Phineas looks up with a wicked smile and shouts at the heavens with a raised fist, "It's game on, bitches!" He sniffs another popper and floors the gas pedal, bull-whipping the seething Ferrari.

Ito bustles down an open Japanese-style wooden stairway.

A bearded man in his thirties drives on the freeway in a pickup truck packed with barrels. His head rocks to the metal music blasting from the radio while he smokes a blunt and scrolls on his cell. He's startled by the helicopter lights as he cruises around a blind turn. The man slams on the brakes, skids, and snaps the wheel to straighten out but overcompensates. The truck flips and crashes into the rail, leaving behind a wake of busted barrels that spray oil along the freeway.

Ito turns left at the bottom of the stairs, passing a waterfall-wall with life-sized brass cranes mingling at the basin pool below.

Phineas flies around the blind turn at over a hundred miles per hour, swerves around a barrel, but loses control on the slick asphalt.

Ito runs along the waterfall-wall and over a wooden indoor koi-pond bridge.

Detective Cole's Charger crashes into a barrel and three-sixties.

Phineas, trapped by the airbag in his smoking, flipped Ferrari, opens his eyes to Cole's mindless vehicle spinning toward him. He screams, *"Ryan!"*

The cars collide and burst into flames as a large, smoldering sun pierces the horizon.

Ito is at the opposite end of the koi-pond bridge and stops at a thick antique door guarded on each side by green, wooden Tara puja statues. Perched above the door's transom is a fierce three-toed jade dragon.

CHAPTER 2

Los Angeles, Around 40 Years Ago

Phineas, at nineteen years old, shines a black wingtip shoe planted on the metal footrest of a weathered shine box. The box has a hand-painted baseball with "LA" scripted above the ball and "Hounds" below it. His pants and Converse sneakers are dotted with holes, and he wears a tattered LA Greyhounds baseball cap and T-shirt.

Phineas talks as he works. "Al Ryan was the last great pitcher the Hounds signed." He finishes buffing with a flourish then taps the polished shoe and a chafed one takes its place. This shoe has a four-inch lifter sole and belongs to Harold Walcott, a white-haired, red-faced octogenarian holding a Fritz-handled cane and wearing a Bogart fedora and a three-piece suit.

Walcott responds, "Their scouts couldn't smell a winner if he was sitting under their noses."

"We'll land another winner one day. Hey, speaking of winners." Phineas pulls a soft cloth from his pocket and opens it to reveal a Morgan silver dollar. "It's slightly worn but it has a slight defect on the date. Right there." Phineas points to the bottom of the coin.

Walcott squints. "I can't see it."

"You can't with the naked eye, but it has a defect on the eight. And, as you know, defects make a thing special... one-of-a-kind." Phineas grins.

"The last coin you sold me was appraised fifty dollars below what I paid for it."

"Of course it was. But how's a man to put food on the table?"

Walcott chuckles. "You're the only guy I know who can screw me, admit it, and convince me to buy more... How much?"

"This one's only seventy-five dollars."

"Any plans for tomorrow?" Walcott asks.

Phineas puts the coin away and gets back to shining. "I'll be right here if it's not raining."

"But nobody needs a shine on New Year's Day!"

"Perhaps," Phineas says, "but it's all about consistency. People know I'm here whether they need my services or not. It's good business."

Walcott points at Phineas. "My son lacks your work ethic because I gave him everything, which is the worst thing a parent can do." The old man sighs. "I thought I was doing right by him, but I created an entitled, drunken gambler. If I could do it over, I'd give him every opportunity to succeed, but after graduation, he'd be cut off – no inheritance either. That'd make him hungry, like you."

Phineas purses his lips. "That's advice I'll be sure to follow, sir. Thank you. That'll be two dollars... or seventy-five dollars flat if you adopt Miss Liberty."

Walcott hands Phineas a one hundred bill. "I think Mr. Franklin will cover it."

"Thank you, sir! Thanks so much!"

The men exchange goods as a limo pulls up at the curb thirty feet away. Walcott winks and trudges away with a hard limp. He looks at Phineas for a few beats before his driver opens the door to a spacious, empty cabin.

Phineas calls out, "Happy New Year, Mr. Walcott."

Walcott waves back before plodding his way into the vehicle.

When the limo pulls away, *Walcott Hotels* can be seen across the street in enormous letters, standing at the base of a glittering skyscraper.

Phineas takes a water-filled Coca-Cola bottle from a satchel under his chair, unscrews the cap, and chugs it.

"Phineas Stone?" asks a garbled voice behind him.

Phineas turn around slowly. "And you are?"

Flashing a badge, the man says, "I'm Detective Cole Simmons, and I need to ask you some questions at the station."

"I can answer all of your questions right here if you like."

Cole snarls, "We could either walk to my car or I can drag you there. Your choice."

"Sir, if I don't work, I don't eat, so—"

Cole slaps a cuff on Phineas' wrist.

"Wait! Am I under arrest? What the hell!"

Ito Hachi paints watercolor bamboo trees on an easel before a handful of students while a trio of young Asian musicians play the calming strings and flutes of traditional Japanese music. Each student stands behind an easel that holds a large sheet of parchment paper. A Japanese woman in her late twenties, wearing a black kimono and holding a baby boy, rushes to Ito and speaks into his ear. Ito drops his brush and dashes away. He runs out of a one-story building

6

displaying a sign that reads, *The Cherry Blossom Japanese Cultural Center*. He walks alongside Phineas, who is being led away by Cole.

"What's happening, Phineas?"

Phineas answers, "I'm not quite sure."

Cole turns toward Ito. "Go eat a fortune cookie and mind your own business, Kato."

Phineas says, "Ito, please grab my stuff."

Ito gathers Phineas' things and runs them to the center, where the Japanese woman stands in the entranceway with her baby.

Cole shoves Phineas into the backseat of a dusty sedan, then sashays around the car, flops into the driver's seat, and pulls away with inane urgency.

Phineas and Cole sit across from each other at a scratched wooden table. Cole's cigarette smoke mixes with the stale air in the depressing, windowless space. The detective stares at Phineas with repugnancy as he unravels the string from a manilla envelope. He then plunks down seven black-and-white, eight-by-ten photos, each one illustrating a different perspective of an open-eyed, unshaven corpse lying on sand. Copious blood leaks from wounds to the temple, neck, and groin.

Cole crushes his cigarette in an ashtray and points at the photos. "This was my first ever homicide. The vic's name is Leo Gates, and he was found mutilated on Venice Beach in a place where you squatted." Cole lights another cigarette then crouches down near Phineas. "If you confess now, I promise you'll get off easy. But if you deny it…" Cole chuckles. "Then the boys at Alcatraz will have years and years of fun with a cute little specimen like you."

Phineas shrugs. "I have no knowledge of this unfortunate

soul, but if I hear anything, I'll be sure to let you know." He touches the side of his nose with his forefinger then straightens his cap and smiles.

Cole speaks through clenched teeth. "A witness places you at the scene."

Phineas responds with a raised brow. "Is that so?"

Cole takes a long pull on his cigarette.

Phineas asks, "Am I under arrest, Detective?"

The two men stare at each other for a few beats before Phineas cuts the silence with, "Didn't think so."

Cole explodes at Phineas, backhanding him with a crushing blow. "You did this, you damned midget!"

Phineas looks at Cole and smiles warmly. "Let it go, Detective."

Cole grunts, "I'll let it go when I see cows fly."

"I believe the expression is... pigs. Wrong barn animal."

"I'm gonna lock you up, freak."

Before walking out, Phineas pauses and dispassionately says, "No... you won't."

CHAPTER 3

Phineas and Ito, both shoeless, kneel on cushions at a *chabudai* table and sip tea in the backroom of the Cherry Blossom Japanese Cultural Center. The cozy room has a ceiling made of slanted cedar boards, a small sink and counter, refrigerator, and an old black stove. A twelve-inch Buddha and an equally sized green Tara puja statue stand together on a window ledge. There are two doors on either side of this space and a few layers of cloth partitions that both separate the back room from the rest of the facility and muffle the sounds of the center's various activates... Activities that presently include a man bellowing commands that trigger the pounding of bare feet on a wood floor and the swish of air punches.

The Japanese woman who alerted Ito to Phineas' encounter with Cole walks in softly and bows slightly as she passes. Her boy is strapped to her back and Ito looks lovingly at the pair as they sweep across the room.

Ito sips tea from his gold *yunomi* cup, then looks across at Phineas. "Should you be worried, Phineas?"

Phineas, focused on Ito's neck tattoos, says, "I've always wondered what the rest of that tattoo is... Are you allowed to show it?"

While removing his shirt, Ito replies, "You watch too many movies."

Ito's torso and sleeved arms have dragons, geishas, snakes, birds, flowers, mountains, suns, and koi fish in vibrant reds, yellows, oranges, greens, and blues that pop from their jet-black background. A blooming cherry-blossom tree, intertwined with a myriad of animals, consumes the entirety of his back.

Phineas' curious, squinting eyes interpret the inked storyboard banding Ito's body. "You're a living masterpiece."

Ito pulls up his pants legs, revealing more artistry.

"I'm absolutely blown away… Was it done in Japan?"

"Yes. It took several years to complete."

Phineas continues gazing as Ito explains, "*Tebori* tattoos are a five-thousand-year-old tradition, where a *horishi* uses a bamboo instrument with thin needles at the tip that he dips in ink pots and pushes under the skin."

"What's something like that go for?"

"Mine totaled around fifty thousand US dollars."

Phineas quips, "At least I'd get mine for half off… Was your center doing better then?"

"God, no. But even as my inheritance dwindles, I wouldn't change a thing."

Ito pours tea into his and Phineas' cups from a black *kyusu* teapot, and Phineas says, "You've given me meals when I had none and a roof over my head on many a rainy night. I'll buy this place for you one day, Ito."

"Well, get rich already!"

"Besides the financial pinch, how painful are teboris?"

Ito smiles. "A man who cannot endure pain isn't a man."

Phineas rolls up his sleeves. "We are kindred spirits, my

friend." Thick, blotchy scars cover Phineas' arms. "I made money as a kid playing chicken with a lighter. I'd smile at those boys as I smelled their skin cook… I learned early on that life is just a mind game."

"Ahh, so you use your size to your advantage."

"That's what the ladies say." Phineas raises his yunomi cup. "May the New Year bring us wealth."

Ito raises his. "And health."

The men clink their cups and sip.

Ito adds, "By the way, Phineas, don't party too much tonight."

"But that's what I do best… And tonight, I've been *hired* to party."

Ito looks at Phineas with a head tilt. "Hired?"

In a humid community hall with creaky floors and the smells of yeasty beer, cigarettes, beef jerky, and Pine-Sol is a room full of rowdy young men who spit their pheromones into the room's stench as they celebrate a combined New Year's Eve and bachelor party. They are focused on the stage where a guy dressed in a Walmart-grade Old Man Time get-up, featuring a baldie cap and white nylon beard, labors across the edge of the stage with his plastic walking-stick and hourglass props. The inebriated herd counts away the final seconds of the year…

"10, 9, 8, 7…"

Two topless girls in their early twenties, dressed only in diapers, rip through the curtains, and push away Old Man Time.

"…6, 5, 4, 3, 2, 1… Happy New Year!"

Phineas, in a large diaper, jumps through the curtains to a cacophony of grunts, cheers, and rippling whistles. One of the revelers pukes on another's back as the girls escort

Phineas to a stained mattress placed in the center of the horde. The girls lay Phineas on his back as the spectators shoulder each other for a better view. Three diapers shoot up from the volcano of delirious youths, giving way to a rise in primeval chanting.

A few hours later Phineas is at the center of a different type of game. Here, he sits with his Hounds hat on backward across from a guy with the physicality of a linebacker, who's referred to as Biggin. Both are in the process of downing enormous mugs of beer with the overflow streaming from their mouths and down their necks. Between Phineas and Biggin are three filled shot glasses. At the table's center is a roll of cash bound by a rubber band. Phineas and Biggin drain the mugs and shoot the shots. Phineas finishes first, grabs the cash, and puts his arms up in triumph.

Biggin punches the bar and growls, "Damn it!" but then looks at Phineas, who's smiling wide. Biggin stares at Phineas for a few beats before bursting into laughter. He then bellows, "Little man!" repeatedly until the whole place echoes the chant.

A car grinds its sidewalls along a curb before knocking over a steel garbage pail and screeching to a stop. Laughter rings out as Phineas exits the vehicle. Biggin's window rolls down. "You're a machine, little man! A fucking machine!"

Phineas replies, "That I am, brother!"

Shouts of, "Later, little man," and other jovial farewells ring out as the car drives away.

Phineas smiles joyfully and waves with both arms until the vehicle is just out of sight. He then runs to the curb and vomits.

Phineas turns into a back alley past a smelly dumpster and approaches a steel door with a sign atop saying *The Regent*

Hotel. He enters a bustling kitchen and sees Archie, a bald man in his early seventies, pushing a cart of towels.

Archie stops when he sees Phineas. "Yo, Phin, we booked solid, bro. So I bagged your stuff and moved you to the janitor's closet."

Phineas impersonates Sylvester Stallone in *Rocky*. "Yo, Archie. I've been coming here for like two years and you put my stuff in a bag on skid row?"

Archie laughs. "That's good, man… You talented!"

"And very available if Sly needs a stunt double." Phineas slips Archie a few bills. "Thanks, Archie."

Archie winks and says, "Happy New Year to ya," before continuing on with his towel cart.

Phineas enters a supply room and walks to a cot with a small basket of toiletries, an apple, and a laundry bag of clothes. He places the items on the floor before plopping wearily onto the cot with a grunt. Just before closing his eyes, he looks up at a wall clock that reads 5:45.

At 8:30 am, Harold Walcott pulls up in a limo to the location where he and Phineas parted the day prior. He's dressed in a three-piece suit and clomps toward Phineas, who energetically opens his folding chair and A-frame sign.

Walcott is approaching from behind, but Phineas turns when he hears Walcott's familiar gait. "Happy New Year, Mr. Walcott! What brings you here at this hour?"

"You! Come with me."

As Walcott limps away, Phineas places a *Be Right Back* sign on his chair, picks up his shine box, and hurries to catch Walcott.

The two men walk through the dimly lit corridor of Walcott's expansive offices, decorated with sturdy wooden furniture, and splashed with whimsical 1960s avant-garde art.

Walcott asks, "If you found a million dollars, what would you do with it?"

"I'd invest it in the most lucrative enterprise known to man."

"And that is?"

"Gambling!" Phineas says with a flare.

"Ha! That's the least lucrative."

"Not for the casino, it isn't."

"Now that's a horse of a different color, my friend."

Phineas presses on. "Because of gambling, casinos can afford to spend millions on trivial commodities like chandeliers and pool tables."

"And how would you compete with the big boys?" Walcott asks.

"I'd both shift the casino atmosphere and bring gambling beyond its few legal provinces. For instance, every hotel I owned within twenty miles of the ocean would have gambling ships that sailed beyond a country's jurisdiction, and it'd be the party of a lifetime – that's the shift I'm talking about. It'd be an adrenaline rush like no other!"

"Why reinvent a tried-and-true formular? Like you said, casinos can spend millions on a light fixture and laugh it off."

"Because I can do it better." Walcott raises an eyebrow and Phineas elaborates. "Most adults live rote, boring lives... every day... day after day... day in... day out. It's a crueler version of prison because they think they're free. People go to the same job they don't want to go to, and do the same tasks they don't want to do and sleep with the same person they don't want to sleep with. I know this because I shine their shoes and they tell me their stories. People long for the party that was their youth, but they're handcuffed to expectations, commitments, and responsibilities."

"You may be on to something." Walcott agrees.

"Mr. Walcott, sir, religion isn't the opium of the masses, repetition is, and people will do anything to relive the apex of their youth through an ass-kicking party and the dream of financial freedom. If I had a million dollars, I'd build an empire."

Walcott presses a button on his keychain, an office door glides open, and he invites Phineas in with a wave of his cane. "And if you were wrong and lost every penny?"

I'd rather take a shot at millions as a young man than work my life away for a time when my biggest thrill is reading Playboy magazine and getting the senior citizen's discount at Shop Rite." Phineas puts down his shine box, jumps into a chair, folds one leg over the other, and asks, "So... are you going to make me an offer?"

"Are you quite sure I'm offering you something?"

"No... but I do know you *don't* want me to make you more of what you already possess. What you want from me is to put the juice back into your life. Isn't that why you invited me here this morning?"

Walcott stares at Phineas for a few beats, rubbing his chin with his index finger. He then points at Phineas, and exclaims, "The first thing you'll need is a real estate license, and I want to show you something I've been working on." He uses his cane to clear a space on the desk, sending objects crashing to the floor. He spreads out plans and Phineas looks on with a slight grin, nodding from time to time as he focuses on Walcott's animated pitch.

CHAPTER 4

Five years later, Phineas, Ito, and Mr. Walcott are at a LA Greyhounds game. A bearded Phineas stands in the seats near the dugout wearing a black tee, beige slacks, Gucci shoes, a gold watch, Ray Bans, and his old Hounds cap. Ito is in an off-white collarless loop-button shirt, karate pants, and black martial-arts shoes. Walcott wears his de rigueur three-piece suit, which is garnished with a white carnation.

Phineas glances left and sees Baxter "Rollie" Rollins signing a program for a female fan, using her back as a standing desk. A cigarette is clenched between his teeth as he writes. Rollie is a tall man in his late thirties with a beer belly, thick Fu Manchu mustache, furry arms, and a shock of wiry ear hair. When finished signing, the girl thanks him with a kiss and Rollie struts away.

Phineas flies out of his row and rushes up the steps.

An old priest holds out a program toward Rollie as he passes, but Rollie waves it away with the back of his hand and it falls to the floor.

On the field, Nelson Hernandez, a giant, two-hundred-twenty-pound Hound walks up to the plate. The catcher,

Brick Jackson – a moniker he earned for his bull-headed persona and his solid physique – says, "Nellie, you walk up here like you on a red carpet."

Nelson settles himself in the box, Brick throws down a sign, and the first pitch comes in.

"Strike!" squawks the umpire.

Nelson answers without looking, "When you're as good as me, you're *always* on a red carpet."

Brick shakes his head. "You one cocky bastard, Nellie."

Phineas catches up to Rollie and says, "Baxter Rollins… I, sir, am your biggest fan… Well, not your *biggest*."

Rollie belly laughs, then stops, snaps his fingers, and points at Phineas. "Wait, you're that playboy with the casino boats."

Nelson Hernandez and Brick Jackson continue their banter at home plate.

Nelson says, "I can afford to be cocky because I hit home runs."

The ball slaps into Brick's glove and the ump screams, "Strike two!"

Nelson continues, "In fact, I'm gonna hit one out now."

Brick snorts. "I bet you dinner at Le Château you ain't hittin' one out."

The next ball comes in and the ump crows, "Ball one."

Nelson says, "You're on, Brick."

"Good, 'cause I'm hungry as hell. You got some nasty-ass eats at this ballpark."

Phineas opens his palms, lifts his chin high, and says, "You are correct, and I am offering you an invitation to party with us tonight on our best ship."

Rollie says, "You, sir, are my kind of guy!"

BORN FOR THE GAME

The crack of a bat jerks Phineas' and Rollie's attention onto the field as they follow the baseball on its journey into the seats behind a billboard featuring a smiling man holding a bottle. Its caption reads *Swiftwater II Liquid Fuel.*

Nelson flips the bat and says to Brick, who is standing there with his mask off, "Hey, Brick, I haven't eaten since last night."

"You are one lucky son of a bitch!"

Phineas and Rollie low-five each other, then Phineas says, "Let me introduce you to some people."

Walcott and Ito are looking toward Phineas as he approaches with Rollie.

"This is Hall of Fame pitcher Baxter Rollins, the greatest knuckleballer ever."

"Damn right. Although these days I'm merely the Hounds' senior scout."

Phineas and Walcott look at each other and smile.

Phineas points to Walcott with an open hand. "This is Harold Walcott."

"Of the Walcott Hotels?" asks Rollie.

"Yes, sir."

Rollie points to Phineas. "I like who ya run with."

"And this is Ito Hachi, founder of the first Japanese Cultural Center in LA."

"That's cool! You do that kung fu stuff?"

Ito shakes his head and says, "Kung fu is a Chinese art."

Phineas jumps in. "Ito is a jujutsu and karate grand master."

Rollie looks puzzled for a beat. "Same difference, no?" He then whistles to a passing server, "Beer and dogs for my friends, here."

Ito gestures *no* and Rollie says, "That's okay, I'll take his."

He slaps his knee and laughs at his own joke.

Phineas winks at a blank-faced Ito.

In the parking lot after the game, Phineas, Rollie, and Walcott stand near the open door of a black limo.

Walcott says, "I'm going with Ito. I'm tired, Phin."

"That's because you've been running with the bulls, my friend."

Walcott nudges Rollie with his elbow. "All the money in the world couldn't buy what Phin has given me."

"What's that?"

A mischievous grin smooths the wrinkles on the old man's face. "A strong finish."

"And there's more to come, Mr. Walcott. I'll see you in the morning." Phin looks in Ito's direction and gives a quick head-bow. "Ito."

Ito returns the head-bow and Phineas closes the door.

Rollie says, "Your boy Ito doesn't talk very much."

A driver opens the door to an adjacent pearl-white limo and Phineas chuckles as he gets in. "You can't shut him up if he likes you."

CHAPTER 5

P hineas and Rollie get out of the limo at a dock near a ramp leading to the Mediterranean Casino Cruise Ship. The magnificent black-and-gold vessel blasts club music as it readies itself for the evening's festivities.

Cole Simmons, wearing a fedora and smoking a cigarette, leans against the ship's ramp, looking away from Phineas until he and Rollie approach. "Good evening, Mr. Stone," says the detective, cordially.

"You're a bit early, Detective, we don't board for at least an hour."

Cole grits his teeth and then does a double take at Rollie. "Baxter Rollins! Hey, man! It's an honor. A real honor to meet you!"

"Did you want an autograph?"

"Sure." Cole hands Rollie a notebook and pen while addressing Phineas. "I spoke to your old friend Art Talbert yesterday."

"How is old Art these days?"

"Not so good, physically, but his mind is razor sharp." Cole gets back his autographed book and shakes Rollie's hand. "Thanks so much, Mr. Rollins."

"Hey, any friend of Phineas is a friend of mine."

Phineas and Cole glance at each other.

Cole says, "Yeah… Hey, Phin, we'll talk again real soon." Cole walks away as Phineas and Rollie climb the ramp.

"Who's Art Talbert?"

"An old foster father of mine who beat and abused children. He had a special affinity for me."

"So why was the dick asking about him?"

"Because I nearly killed Talbert around twenty-five years ago."

"Why's that?"

"One night, when Talbert came home drunk, as was his routine, I was waiting for him behind a lilac bush in the side yard. When he came wobbling by, I hit him over the head with a shovel, then beat him bloody. When I was done, I wiped my hands on his shirt and hit the road for good. I was sixteen."

Rollie says with a broad smile, "I liked you from the get-go!"

Several hours later, the boat is cruising along the black ocean. Thumping music and a techno lightshow pulse from an upper dance floor. The gaming area below is loud and festive with bells, laughter, and a barrage of flashing slot-machine lights. Phineas and Rollie are on the gaming floor surrounded by six models and a crowd of onlookers. Phineas sniffs a popper, throws the dice, and the crowd cheers. Rollie follows suit then grabs a tray of Jell-O shots from a passing waitress. He, Phineas, and the models suck them down like oysters. A tall blonde from Phineas' entourage lies back on a cocktail table, puts two Jell-O shots on her belly and points at Phineas and Rollie who suck them off to a crescendo of cheers.

Rollie shouts, "You know how to party, my dude!"

"We do this every night!" Phineas grabs a mic, flicks a

switch, and the sound fades on the ship. He shouts into the mic, "Ladies and gentlemen, all drinks are double alcohol and free for an hour!" A huge clock lights up with numbers reading "60:00." The seconds roll back, the crowd cheers, and the sound returns to the rapt club.

In Phineas' private cabin, he and Rollie sit in leather chairs, sip bourbon from snifters, and smoke Cubans. Phineas' custom chair is fitted to his stature.

Rollie lifts a crystal liquor decanter and portions out booze to both glasses with a generous hand. "The day I was enshrined in the Hall of Fame was my best day, and it's been a steep plunge ever since."

Phineas blows a smoke ring that floats away like a ghost before it wiggles and dissipates. "I wanted to be a pro ball-player from the time I was this high." He reaches down from his chair, his hand a few inches off the red maple floor. Rollie chuckles and Phineas waxes on, "I have the burn so bad I can feel it in my bones… I'm like Tantalus in Hades who stands famished and parched in a pool of water beneath fruit trees, yet the fruit rises as he reaches for it and the water drains when he tries to drink. I'd trade the money, the cars, the yachts, and the women to play in the major leagues for minimum wage."

Rollie nods. "I don't know who Tantalus is, but I get it, man. My dad was a prized minor-league pitcher in the Reds' organization, but when his father died, he had to quit baseball to support his mother. They say the booze killed him, but I know that it was the suffocated dream that did him in."

"One of my dads, Stan Kaminski, was a man in his late seventies whose three loves were the Los Angeles Greyhounds, the US Marine Corps, and Jack Daniels… in that order, and the first game he brought me to, Al Ryan pitched his perfect game."

"You were there? Wow! Unbelievable! That was the most dominant performance in the history of the sport... Twenty-three strikeouts. Ryan was a beast."

Phineas tops off their glasses. "He was everything I wanted to be – tall, strong, confident, with unbridled talent. Ryan was my hero... Still is, actually. I always found it to be serendipitous that my foster dad Stan Kaminski and Al Ryan died on the same day a few years apart. One of my biggest let-downs in life was that I only got to live with Stan for eighteen months. He died minutes after the Hounds won the pennant. We did a shot of Jack, I went to the bathroom, and when I came back, he was slumped over in his recliner."

Rollie raises his glass. "To Stan Kaminski." The men gulp and Rollie parcels out more of the amber libation. "What was your real dad like?"

"Don't know, but my guess is that he was a pro ball-player who got some whore pregnant."

Rollie laughs.

"No, I mean it. It's like this... Your dad was a pitcher and you were too. It's all in the blood. In the animal kingdom, females choose specific males to create superior offspring. Humans mate based on who has a nice car and the outcome is a crapshoot. Matching superior traits creates a superior individual."

Rollie blows out smoke. "I think Hitler tried that."

"Hitler wanted to create a master race and take over the world. I merely want to create the perfect baseball player."

"You—" Rollie's response is stilled by knocking.

Phineas looks at the door. "Yes?"

A voice answers, "I have your phones, sir."

Phineas looks at his Rolex and says, "It's open, Gus."

A man with dwarfism hands Phineas and Rollie their phones.

Phineas gives Gus a tip then looks at his cell. "Rollie, you'll have to get a cab home."

A few hours later, Phineas walks into a hospital room where Walcott is attached to a hash of tubes and machines.

Perry Walcott, Harold's sixty-year-old son, stained with yellowy eyes and skin, looks at Phineas with contempt. "What the fuck are you doing here? I guarantee that whoever let you in will be fired!"

Mr. Walcott begins bucking, his machines cry out, and a stream of medical personnel pours into the room.

As a nurse escorts Phineas and Perry out, Perry looks at Phineas and says, "My father will be dead soon and I am his sole heir. I hope you saved your shine box."

CHAPTER 6

Detective Cole sits on his couch watching TV and eating lo mein with a plastic fork from a take-out container. A cigarette burns in an ashtray next to a beer on a tray-table.

He flips the TV on with the remote and sees a photo of Phineas and Walcott. The off-screen anchor reports, "Billionaire real-estate mogul Harold Walcott bequeaths the five-hundred-million-dollar Mediterranean Hotel and Casino chain to business partner and international playboy Phineas Stone. Harold Walcott, who grew his father's small real-estate company into an international hotel chain, died a week ago from a sudden heart attack at the age of ninety-seven. He leaves behind a son, Perry Walcott, who is presently contesting his late father's will."

Rollie sits on his recliner smoking a cigarette and eating Mallomars as the news broadcast about Walcott and Phineas plays on his TV. The ESPN theme song sounds on Rollie's cell and he clicks it on. "Yeah?"

A flat voice answers, "They want their money tonight."

Rollie takes a drag of his cigarette, and pleads, "Just one more bet and I'm gonna be in the black. Put five grand on

Sport Coat tomorrow. It's a sure thing."

The voice responds, "Okay, Rollie, but this is the last time. Oh, and I'll be by in a little bit. I want your three-hundredth career ball for the favor." A dial tone sounds.

Rollie looks back at the TV where there's a photo of Phineas and Walcott wearing captain hats in front of a row of slot machines. Rollie taps his cell a few times. "Hey, Phin. How goes it, brother?"

In the same dingy LAPD interrogation room where Phineas and Cole sat over a decade ago, Phineas, in a Hawaiian shirt, shorts, and flip-flops, is next to his attorney, Kim Biles, a woman in her thirties wearing a black Fendi skirt suit. They are across from detective Cole and his bald superior.

Kim eyes the men with rancor. "Another frivolous, unjustified incident between my client and detective Cole will result in a very public, very deprecating, very expensive lawsuit. We'll paint the LAPD as a bastion of discrimination and publicly donate our settlement to victims of disability discrimination."

Cole snaps, "But this man—"

The bald superior cuts in, "I promise that detective Cole will stand down."

"I'm glad we are clear," says Ms. Biles as she and Phineas walk away.

As they approach the door, Phineas says, "It's funny, Ms. Biles, but I saw a flock of cows fly over my house this morning."

"Cows?"

Cole's upper lip curls as he points at the vacant doorway. "She can't do damned a thing, because—"

"Cole! What the hell is wrong with you? You're harassing

a millionaire mogul about the death of a homeless predator that no one gives a rat's ass about. If you continue this witch hunt, you'll be discharged."

The superior exits the room and Cole stares at the chair where Phineas sat, then puts his fingers into the shape of a gun, points it at the chair, and shoots it, making bullet sounds, *pfff, pfff, pfff.* He lights a cigarette and sits in Phineas' chair.

CHAPTER 7

P hineas, in a dragon kimono, and Rollie, in rubber flip-flops and a zippered white-and-blue terrycloth jacket, walk down the same staircase that Ito raced down at the beginning of the story.

Phineas says, "Sorry for the delay, but I had some LAPD business."

"Problems with your dick friend?"

"Dick problems? Never." They pass the waterfall-wall with the brass cranes at the base, to a door through which they exit. Phineas and Rollie walk onto a patio where there are three beauties in a round infinity pool. Phineas points to the girls. "And that, my friend, is why."

A girl shouts, "Are we playing volleyball?"

"Only if we play at the shallow end," responds Phineas.

The girls laugh and Rollie looks at Phineas. "Oh, how I ever like who ya run with."

The patio has slate walkways, a wooden bridge, hot springs, cabanas, and foliage in various shapes and colors accented by pruned bonsai and cherry blossom trees. The men walk to a table where Ainu, an Asian female in a kimono, joggles a bartender shaker.

They sit and Phineas says, "Good afternoon, Ainu. This is my friend Rollie Baxter."

Ainu pours a cloudy pink mixture into ice-filled rock glasses. "Good afternoon, sir." She gives a quick head bow and Rollie reciprocates. She places two domed food trays on the table and removes the lids. One has lobster chunks on shaved ice and the other has steaming, cubed filet mignon. Each has tongs and a silver tray of dipping sauce. She places a silver plate and fork in front of each of them and bows her head.

Phineas says, "Thanks so much, Ainu," and she walks to a space just out of earshot.

Rollie takes a sip, swallows, and then gulps down another mouthful. "That's excellent."

Phineas says, "Yes. Ainu is magic."

"Hey, Phin, I'm real sorry about Mr. Walcott."

"Thank you, Rollie. He was like a father to me."

"You had a lot of fathers."

"Indeed... So, what brings you here, another night on the Mediterranean?"

Rollie downs the rest of the drink and wipes his mouth with the back of his hand. "What you said that night on the ship about creating the perfect baseball player... I've been thinking about it ever since."

"I've been thinking about it ever since Al Ryan pitched that perfect game."

Ainu refills their glasses.

"I'm your man, Phin! I have the experience, talent, and MLB connections to pull this off."

Phineas takes a sip of his drink and looks at Rollie for a beat. "That you do, and you're at least half as crazy as I am."

Rollie says, "I'd say a little more than half," as he spears a few chunks of the charred, pink beef.

Phineas spoons lobster into his plate. "I'd be lying if I said I haven't been thinking about you in this regard since we met. However, there'd be... protracted conditions... A twenty-year commitment, to be precise, and you must follow my plan to the letter – no negotiations, no questions asked. And, Rollie, even if we were to come to terms, it would all depend on Ito."

"Why Ito?"

"Because he'd be the boy's main parent. God knows I'm too much of an asshole to raise him."

Rollie nods. "Well, I'm all the hell in. I'll go along with everything you want – no questions asked... Except one... Will I get a signing bonus?"

"Absolutely!" Phineas says with vigor.

"When do we start?"

A volleyball bounces off Phineas' head and the girls cackle. "Let's play, Phinny!"

"She's right! Let's play, and I'll talk to Ito in the morning."

Rollie raises his drink. "To the greatest baseball player of all time."

Phineas says, "To Ryan!"

They swallow their drinks and Phineas calls out, "Ainu, have a few cases of Dom Pérignon brought out and invite the whole staff into the pool. They may join us either with or without their swimsuits!"

Ainu giggles coyly, bows, and exits in haste.

The three beauties grab Phineas and Rollie and run them into the pool.

CHAPTER 8

Phineas leans on a post of the koi-pond bridge. Behind him is the rustic doorway adorned with the Tara puja and dragon statues that Ito stopped and stared at just before the flashback began.

Ito feeds large, speckled koi from a wicker basket. He looks up at Phineas. "Not with Rollie... There's something off about him."

"I admit that the man is flawed, but aren't we all? He brings a Hall of Fame career to the table, he's well connected, and he wants to do it."

"But does he want to do it for the same reasons as you?"

"I don't know," responds Phineas with a shrug, "but he's hungry, and I need that if this is going to work."

"If I accept... I'd have to close the center."

Phineas nods a few times before responding, "I understand that it was your and Hana's dream... I do. But the accident was many years ago, Ito. Maybe this is a new beginning – a new dream. Plus, you could keep the center going if you want, and start a new life here."

Ito looks up from the fish. "Here?"

"I'll build you a sanctuary and you could do the things

with our boy that you would have done with your son. You can bring him to Japan, teach him your ways, martial arts… Be the father you wanted to be."

"It wasn't meant for me."

Phineas walks along the pond's edge and contemplates a bonsai bush. "If you believe that, then you must consider the possibility that you and I were cheated and the universe is making amends for taking your family from you and imprisoning me in this wretched body. Your acceptance means I get a chance to be a part of the person I always dreamed of being, but one thing is for sure – I cannot do it without you."

Ito leans toward Phineas. "And if you are wrong and we tempt fate?"

Phineas raises his chin. "Against you and me? Fate ain't got a chance in hell."

Ito looks at Phineas for a beat, sucks in a long breath, then looks at the koi who wait, open- mouthed, like baby birds.

CHAPTER 9

The mansion's conference room is located on the second floor of the east wing. It has large windows on the exterior wall with views of beautifully trimmed trees and a flowing brook saddled with arched bridges. The rectangular room has a long table with ten chairs on each side and Phineas' telescoping chair at the head. Today, however, Ito, Rollie, and Phineas are the only attendees. Phineas stands on a platform approximately fifteen feet from the conference table. Behind him is a large screen displaying an image of Babe Ruth. Phineas gestures to the image. "And then there's Babe Ruth... the greatest of them all." Phineas clicks a remote and Ruth's statistics appear. He reads them aloud:

714 home runs
342 batting average
2,873 hits
94-46 pitching record
2.28 ERA.

Phineas continues, "Ruth was the greatest in the game, but

Ryan will be better."

He taps his remote and a video plays scratchy footage of the Babe hamming it up for the camera.

"Ruth smoked, drank, partied, ate hot dogs, and was dead at fifty-three. Ryan will not even peak at fifty-three. The Bambino had two factors that created his legend – talent and mystique. Ryan's talent will come from carefully chosen parents, which will be enhanced by the preparation and training that has already begun. Ryan's mystique will come from the surprise."

Rollie cocks an eyebrow.

Phineas frees nervous energy by pacing back and forth across the platform. "Ryan's training will begin twenty-three weeks after conception. The child will be 'spoken to' in the womb, through classical music and the sounds of baseball games… sounds that will continue for months following the birth." He clicks and reads off the screen:

- Baseball images will surround the nursery through mobiles, posters, sheets, etc.
- Looping baseball videos will play on TVs throughout the house and in the nursery. Ryan will sleep to the sounds of baseball games.
- Ryan will be given baseballs to grip made in proportionate size and weight to hand growth and strength.
- All infant and toddler games will be designed with a specific purpose. There will be, for example, hand-eye coordination activities, such as popping bubbles or switching items from hand to hand.
- Whatever is done with one hand is done with the other. Ryan will be ambidextrous.

- Ryan will live by the polyphasic sleep pattern, or Uberman Cycle, consisting of a hybrid of three hours of sleep and two hours of meditation/rest. Leonardo da Vinci, Nikola Tesla, Thomas Edison, Salvador Dali, Buckminster Fuller, and other icons lived by this cycle.

The screen changes.

Ryan's Basic Life-Sleep Schedule:

12:00 am – 2:00 am (sleep 2 hours)
2:00 am – 6:00 am (awake 4 hours)
6:00 am – 6:30 am (.5 hour of relaxation)
6:30 am – 11:30 am (awake 5 hours)
11:30 am – 1:30 pm (sleep 2 hours)
1:30 pm – 6:30 pm (awake 5 hours)
6:30 pm – 7:30 pm (1 hour of relaxation)
7:30 pm – 12 am (awake 4.5 hours)
Hours of Sleep Per 24: 4
Hours of Rest Per 24: 1.5
Hours of Activity Per 24: 18.5

Eating:

- Ryan will eat several organic mini-meals throughout a 24-hour cycle, so there will be no heavy digestion periods.

Yearly Cycle:

Cycle 1: March – October
(8 months of baseball and academics.)

BORN FOR THE GAME

Cycle 2: November
(1 month of meditation, yoga, and academics.)
Cycle 3: December – January
(2 months of martial arts, gymnastics, and academics.)
Cycle 4: February
(1 month of meditation, yoga, and academics.)

- Stretching and Meditating Daily
- During cycles 1 and 3, there are 30-60 mins of stretching and meditation per day.
- During Cycles 2 and 4, there are 3-5 hours of stretching and meditation per day. There is also time for movies/TV during cycles 2 & 4.
- Female Influence
- Ballet/gymnastics teacher
- Piano teacher
- Some educators

Secrecy:

- Everyone who works with Ryan will be paid well and contractually bound to silence.
- Ryan's biological parents will not be revealed nor will they have any influence or contact for a minimum of twenty-five years. Ryan will not know of this stipulation.

"Academics will be privately taught here by the best educators in the world. Athletic training will also be privately coached here by pros of baseball, martial arts, and gymnastics. Everything we do, every aspect of Ryan's life, will be done in secret."

Phineas closes his eyes and smiles through his next reveal. "At nineteen, Ryan walks onto the field an unknown, no history or scouting report available, and nine innings later, walks off an international superstar."

Rollie stands. "Are you kidding? No! No! You've got this part wrong. Ryan must play with other boys through Little League, travel teams, and run through single, double, and triple A farm teams. I'm sorry, Phineas, but I know what I'm talking about here and your plan is a fantasy. It can't be done."

Phineas shoots back, "There is no can't, because no one has ever done what we are going to do. We sail in uncharted waters. Our plan will be our mantra." He clicks the remote. "Secrecy... MLB at 19... Best Ever."

Rollie shakes his head then looks at Ito, who looks back at him, stone faced.

Phineas changes the image to a picture of a man in his fifties smiling on a billboard ad, holding a bottle, with the caption *Swiftwater II Liquid Fuel*. "Ryan's father will be Dakota Swiftwater."

Rollie smacks the table. "I told you he'd do it!" He points to Ito. "He's a good friend of mine."

Ito asks, "Is he a baseball player? I thought he sold sports drinks."

"Are you kidding? He's a Hall of Fame pitcher who hit thirty-eight home runs."

Ito responds, "So, he's like Masaichi Kaneda."

"Who?"

"400 wins: 365 complete games: 82 shutouts: 4,500 strikeouts and he had 406 hits and 38 home runs. He's a legend."

"Where? Japan?" Rollie chuckles and shakes his head.

Phineas regains the floor when he plays a video of

Swiftwater pitching and then hitting an upper-deck home run. "Besides being a Hall of Fame pitcher who slugged the most home runs, as Rollie mentioned, he has a genius IQ of 160. After baseball, he became an Olympic archer." A video streams of Swiftwater on a podium having a medal placed over his head. "At seventy-seven, he still competes in triathlons and Ironman competitions. This is him now." A photo appears of a bald, shirtless, ripped Dakota.

A line sprouts from beneath Dakota's photo to a photo of Satanta Swiftwater, a Native American man in his thirties. A vintage video plays of him riding a horse while throwing knives around a woman in front of an applauding audience.

Phineas adds, "Dakota's father, Satanta, was a Kiowa Indian and circus performer. I found an old playbill from one of his performances saying he could throw a stiletto knife directly into the hole of a wedding ring from over thirty feet away."

Another line grows from under Dakota's photo to a picture of a fair-skinned, dark-haired woman with full lips in her early twenties. A video begins of her flipping through a trapeze routine in the center ring of a circus. "Satanta's wife, Alla Yudovich, came from generations of trapeze artists. The two met at the circus and had Dakota. While Dakota signed up shortly after we met, Ryan's future mother required rounds of negotiations. Concessions were made and I'm thrilled to announce that she signed the contracts yesterday."

Rollie asks, "Is it Sheila Craig?"

Phineas smiles, clicks the remote, and the photo of a beautiful, ecstatic young woman draped in an Italian flag appears. Her smooth spandex suit accentuates thick, muscular legs. She's on a podium with medals around her neck. Valentina Fermi, twenty, has black hair, olive skin, high cheek bones, and neon-blue eyes.

Rollie shouts, "Valentina Fermi? … 'Legs' Fermi? Damn, Phineas! How did you get to her?"

Ito says, "I've seen her."

Rollie, with his hands in the air, gasps, "She's only the most famous Olympic champion ever. People used to say that her legs could crush a cobblestone like a walnut."

Phineas adds, "And besides an array of skating medals, she's the only person to ever win gold medals in both the Winter and Summer Olympics. She won the 500m speed skating and 50m freestyle swim competitions. And if that's not enough, she's related to physicist Enrico Fermi, and her IQ is 1—fucking—95!"

Ito says, "I haven't seen her for years."

Phineas walks slowly toward the lip of the platform as he speaks. "At the height of her career, she lost her right leg at the hip in a motorcycle accident. She's since developed a billion-dollar software company in Turin and disappeared from the public eye. This is a rare video taken of her a few years ago." A video shows Valentina in a short black dress, clumping by in high heels. Her hard plastic prosthetic is shaped to the dimensions of a human leg and painted like stained glass.

Phineas clicks the remote and a branch stretches down from Valentina to a blonde and blue-eyed woman with overly muscular legs. She's posing with several medals around her neck and fistfuls more in each hand.

"Valentina's mother, Greta Albina, was a champion figure skater from the Italian city of Aosta, which sits on the Swiss border."

"Isn't Valentina's father an Olympian, too?" Rollie asks.

A line stretches from Valentina to a tall, black-haired man

holding a soccer ball.

"That's correct. Valentino Fermi was an Olympic soccer player who later became a physicist."

"What was Valentina's issue?"

"We worked through several, but there were two big ones. The original contract stated that the parents would never see Ryan, but I compromised by adding a twenty-five-year term. The main bone of contention, however, was the in-vitro process, which is invasive, and Valentina will not lose control of her fertilized eggs. She's a celebrity and wary of outsiders. She'll only conceive if it's done naturally. 'The way God intended' was her exact phrase."

Rollie slaps his knee. "Dakota is one lucky son of a – wait... We couldn't guarantee a boy!"

"My original thought as well," says Phineas with a grin, "but everything about Ryan has been calculated. I decided that something had to be left to fate."

"Brilliant," exclaims Ito.

"No! It's not *brilliant*! There's nothing *brilliant* about it. A girl is not strong enough. She'd never have the arm strength or bat speed to compete with men, let alone be better than them." Phineas looks away as Rollie continues, "There's a reason why women don't play pro ball and I am the only authority in the room who could speak on that. It's simply not possible!"

"Is something not possible just because it hasn't been done?" asks Phineas.

"Some things are just common sense, Phin."

Ito looks at Phineas and says, *"Hontōni kare to issho ni kore o yaritaidesu ka?"* (Are you sure you want to do this with him?)

Phineas smiles at Ito for a beat and then looks back at Rollie. "People have always made such statements, and they are repeatedly proven wrong. If you're on my team you may never say 'impossible' or 'can't,' and I need to know right now." Phineas takes out two sets of papers. "If you sign this one," Phineas places a folder on the table to Rollie's right, "I give you fifty thousand dollars for your confidentiality, we continue our friendship, and never speak of this again. If you sign this one," Phineas places a folder to Rollie's left, "you're all in. And I can have nothing less than *all*. This is my endeavor and it must be followed without questions."

Phineas clicks the remote. The name Ryan Stone appears at the center of the screen and branches grow from below the name to connect Valentina Fermi and Dakota Swiftwater, completing the family tree.

Phineas looks at Rollie and says, "Secrecy, MLB at 19, best ever." He tosses Rollie a pen.

CHAPTER 10

The Present

A panting, perspiring Ito stands staring at the rustic door. Instrumental yoga music seeps out from inside. He steps forward, compresses the thumb-latch handle, and pushes the door open.

The room has knotty pine floors and the glass walls to the right of the doorway reveal the outdoor section of the koi pond that is hemmed in by a cluster of Japanese maples. A twenty-five-foot gold Buddha smiles from above an altar opposite the rustic door. Between the door and the Buddha is the back of a girl who stands five feet eleven inches tall. She is wearing black spandex shorts and a black sports bra. Her raven-colored hair is in a tight braid that falls just below her mid-back.

Brightly colored *irezumi* tattoos pop from within their black background. They begin on the bridge of her left foot, flow over her middle toe, under her sole, rise up her Achilles, and cover the back side of her left leg. The graphics snake around her left hip and onto her back, which features the fierce images of a tiger on the left sizing up a dragon on the right. The art rolls over her right shoulder with lines running up the side of her neck and flowing behind her ear and under her jaw. It fully sleeves her right arm, with extensions branching into her armpit and under the right cup of her bra. The tattoo covers the back of her hand, flows over the inside of her middle finger, and ends as a scorpion on her palm. The cast of characters, besides the aforementioned tiger and dragon, are a tapestry of birds, koi fish, snakes, samurai, geishas, mountains, rivers, stars, bonsai, cherry-blossom trees, and the sun.

Her muscles flex and ripple through tai-chi-type movements. Her thick, muscular legs anchor her to the floor without the slightest wiggle as she moves like a human praying mantis through rhythmic combinations.

Ryan turns around as Ito approaches. Her grandmother's ice-blue eyes shine as though backlit against her parents' dark olive skin. Her large, crimson lips and high cheekbones complete an arrangement of unearthly beauty. She's wearing a diamond-covered, heart-shaped, white-gold locket. She cringes while Ito talks. She asks questions and motions for them to leave, but Ito shakes his head and speaks again, calming her.

She takes a deep breath, closes her eyes, then looks up, placing her hand on her chest. After a beat, she turns and walks to the peaceful, smiling Buddha. She kneels and joins her hands while her lips move and she looks up at the golden statue. She closes her eyes and bows with her forehead touching the floor.

Ito joins her as they move up and down in prayer.

A week later, people enter the Buddha room and mingle as mourners do, with soft shoulders, hushed voices, and close to loved ones. A black-robed Asian monk is at the altar lighting incense and candles with a long, thin taper. A framed photo of Phineas faces the congregation. Kim Biles sits with Ainu, who dabs her eyes with a tissue. They are up front near Ito, who dons a black silk kimono, and Ryan, wearing a black lacy dress. Ryan's locket and eyes glint as she scans the room, shakes her head, then turns to look at Phineas' photo. After a few beats, the photo blurs as she reminisces…

Ryan is seven years old and wears a Hounds cap that has her short ponytail sticking out from the sizing hole at the back. She stands on the mansion's baseball field alongside Phineas, who is dressed in a suit and carrying a briefcase, and Rollie, who is smoking. The field is built to the exact dimensions of Greyhound Stadium. Phineas looks lovingly at Ryan who says, "Secrecy, MLB at nineteen, best ever!"

He puts out his hand and Ryan slaps him five. "You make Daddy very happy. And do you know what would make Daddy even happier?"

"What?"

"If Uncle Rollie would listen as well as you do, and not smoke in your presence."

Ryan looks at Rollie and smiles, lovingly.

Rollie flicks the red tip off the cigarette, puts the butt in his pants pocket, and makes a silly face by rolling his eyes up and sticking out his tongue.

Ryan giggles then says, "Uncle Rollie says I might join a baseball tournament this fall."

Phineas responds, "Now, that doesn't sound much at all like secrecy, does it?"

Ryan shakes her head.

"I think Uncle Rollie is just testing you." Phineas turns toward Rollie. "Is that it, Rollie?"

Rollie, with slight animosity, says, "You know me… the

tester." He then looks at Ryan and winks.

Ryan smiles. "Uncle Rollie!"

"Before I leave," says Phineas, "I want to see your best knuckleball."

"Okay. But first I want to show you something, Daddy!"

While Ryan jogs to a tee at home plate, Phineas gives Rollie a stern look before focusing back on Ryan.

Ryan measures the ball with her bat, lifts a leg, and launches it to the middle of the outfield.

Phineas and Rollie clap.

A few hours later, Cole Simmons' photo appears on a large flatscreen in a dark office. Below Cole's photo is a flag-covered casket that is being carried past a row of white-gloved, saluting officers.

A bushy-browed reporter touches his earpiece with two fingers and speaks into a mic. "We are live at St. Luke's Church in Los Angeles as LAPD Detective Cole Simmons is being laid to rest after burning to death in his vehicle during a freeway collision with billionaire Phineas Stone."

The screen changes to a still photo of Phineas above a video of a Buddhist cemetery.

Ryan, wearing a black birdcage veil, walks with Ito among a small clutch of grievers.

Rollie, who now has a salt-and-pepper flavoring to his hair, stands in front of the flatscreen, focusing on Ryan.

The reporter continues, "Detective Simmons was investigating Stone for the grisly 1970s murder of a Venice Beach homeless man. Detective Simmons, a forty-five-year veteran, was not married and has no children or heirs."

Ryan and Ito enter the mansion and walk into the grand foyer wearing their funeral attire.

Kim Biles is behind them, holding a small, brass, cottage-shaped urn and whispering to her cell.

Ryan removes her veil. "It's unforgivable that Uncle Rollie didn't come!"

"Unforgivable is a strong word, Ryan."

"Yes, it is. Were my parents there?"

Ito shakes his head.

"You wouldn't tell me if they were."

"That's true." He chuckles. "But off the record, they were not."

"Are we still keeping a record?"

Kim hands Ryan the brass cottage. "I'll be right back."

Ryan sits and places the brass cottage on a table constructed of bamboo and glass. "It would have been nice to have had a mother the past week."

"Yes," Ito says. "It would have been."

"I used to think about her a lot when I was a kid. I wondered what she looked like and fantasized that she'd appear when I needed her most. I'd say, 'thank you, Mom' or, 'I love you, Mom.' I wanted to be able to say that... Mom, I mean."

"You never mentioned this before."

"I never lost my father before."

Ito says, "Yes... The loss of a loved one dredges up copious buried emotions."

"What was she like, Ito...? My mom? Was she beautiful?"

"Have you not looked in the mirror, child?"

"I could look like my father."

"True... but your mother is very present in you."

"What was my father like?"

"Strong, dynamic, handsome." He thinks for a beat. "Always smiling..." Ito touches the cottage. "That's a wonderful urn, by the way. Your father would approve."

"It has an incense chimney." Ryan smiles. "When the incense burns, it looks as though someone's home." She removes the cottage roof, which reveals four canisters. She touches each one as she refers to it. "I asked them to divide Daddy's ashes in four. I'll scatter this one at Greyhound Stadium on my first day. This one will go under Daddy's favorite cherry blossom. This'll be buried with my ashes when I die, and this last one will be made into a diamond."

"A diamond?" Ito asks.

"Yes. Can you believe it? There's a place in town that can turn ashes into a diamond..." Ryan smiles. "If I know Daddy, he'd say..." She impersonates Phineas. "'They should've charged you half price for these ashes.'"

Ito responds, "No. He'd probably say there would be an upcharge after they saw his penis."

Ryan explodes laughing, which sets Ito off laughing as well. Ryan gains enough breath to speak through her laughter. "Yes... He... would have said that! That's exactly what he would have said." She wipes tears from the corners of her eyes. "My God, Daddy was so bad!"

Ito says, "And so good. And so funny."

Ryan adds, "How about when he would put a rubber band on the sink sprayer so when someone opened the faucet, the water would hit them in the face!" She and Ito laugh more.

Ryan is laughing so hard she cannot talk. "Remember... Rem..." She laughs again, then catches her breath. "Remember... when Daddy ran into your room that night and said I was in trouble and the two of you ran out..." More laughter... "and he had a piece of... Saran Wrap... across the doorway... He ran under it, but you hit into it with your face and fell on the floor in your boxers." They are both belly-laughing.

Ito says, "And he put some kind of slime on it too... He was such a child."

Kim enters the room, smiles briefly, and then looks somber. She pulls up a chair and Ryan and Ito wipe away their laughing tears before focusing on Kim.

Ryan says, "We were just talking about how funny Daddy was."

Kim smiles wide. "I have a few doozies myself. He literally made me laugh one time while I was presenting at an executive board meeting. I was mortified. I told him I'd have his head if he ever did that again, but, of course, he did it again." Ms. Biles changes her expression and asks, "Ryan, do you know of any money your father may have set aside for you?"

"No," Ryan explains. "He said that was his greatest gift to me. He gave me all the tools to succeed, so the day I turned pro I'd be ready to make my own way in the world, and I will see that through, Ms. Biles."

Kim smiles and turns to Ito. "Do you have any stocks, savings, CDs?"

"No. Phineas bought my center and provided me with everything I needed to live. He offered a salary but I declined. Why do you ask?"

Kim waits a few beats and then says, "Phin is bankrupt."

Ito asks, "Bankrupt?"

Kim continues, "As I'm sure you know, he was building a luxury casino on each of the seven continents that were to open this New Year's Eve, but his under-ocean transport company collapsed last week... Everything is lost."

Ryan asks, "Everything? Our home, too?"

Kim nods. "I've not said all. Detective Simmons had the homeless man's body exhumed and retested... Phin's DNA was very present."

Ryan stands. "No way! That detective must have planted it there—"

Ito interjects, "I cannot thank you enough for your services, Ms. Biles. Phineas both respected and adored you. You will be greatly missed."

"Thank you, Ito. I was very fond of Phineas. He was a good man, and I'm so sorry my news has added weight to your bereavement. I'll take care of everything related to this business, pro bono." Kim shakes Ito's and Ryan's hands with wet, apologetic eyes. "Please take a moment together. I will see myself out."

Ito walks with Ryan, who cradles the urn like a puppy, along a mansion corridor. Muscle memory guides Ryan's course as her brain spins with circular thoughts.

Ito says, "We'll move into the center."

Ryan headshakes herself out of her funk. "The center?"

"Yes. Your father spent many a night there in his homeless days." They stop at a door and Ito says, "We'll talk more tomorrow. You've had a difficult—"

"I want to know, Ito… Right now." Ito and Ryan lock eyes and Ryan says, "Enough of the secrets. I have a right to know."

Ito takes a deep breath, then nods. "Okay… You're right, Ryan… Your father was preyed upon by that homeless man while sleeping on Venice Beach… a place he lived for a few years. During the struggle, your father took out his equalizer – a push-dagger in his boot – and killed the man."

"But it was self-defense. Why didn't he explain that?"

"I'm not sure, but that was your father's choice, and some decisions, good or bad, can affect the trajectory of an entire life."

"It seems he made a pretty bad choice."

"Perhaps," Ito says with a shrug. "But either well-planned or impulsive, decisions are always affected by chance, mood… or the direction of the wind. Your father taught me that. He was one of the greatest people I ever knew."

Ryan forces a smile. "Thank you, Ito. I appreciate you telling me."

"You've been so strong through this, and I commend you."

They bow to each other and Ryan enters her bedroom. She carefully closes the door, places the urn down on the bed, and bolts across the room into her closet. She closes the door, rips a bunch of clothes off of hangers and screams into them with raspy bursts, then sobs as she says, "Oh, Daddy! Daddy!" Ryan takes a gasping breath and asks, "Why? Why? Why?" The final 'why' is loud and long and ends as a throat-shredding scream. Ryan's tears flow from the place in the soul harboring its purest fear and love. She folds into the fetal position, bucking with long, scratchy sobs that subside, but then rise again until exhaustion eventually silences her with sleep. Her body allays into the rhythmic rise and fall of her chest against the floor.

Ryan, Phineas, Ito, Rollie, and Ainu are singing the final line of the birthday song. They wear glittery, coned hats and sit around a table near the mansion's pool that's strewn with gifts and shredded wrapping paper. A cake with candles says Happy 13th Birthday, Ryan!

Ryan blows out the candles and Rollie jumps in with, "Are ya one? Are ya two?"

Ryan giggles, "Uncle Rollie!"

Phineas removes a square, gold-wrapped box from his jacket pocket and hands it to Ryan.

"Wow! Another one?" exclaims Ryan.

With a raised chin and tall shoulders, Phineas says, "This one is very special."

Ryan unwraps it and reads a handwritten message on the box top, "To Ryan, My Diamond." She looks up at Phineas with a child's loving smile, then removes the box top and sees her diamond locket. "It's so beautiful." She gently touches its surface then takes the locket out, flips it over, and reads the inscription on the back. "Love, Daddy."

She clicks it open and Phineas says, "It's empty now, but one day you'll choose something very special to place inside of it."

Ryan kisses the open locket. "You will always be inside, Daddy." She squeezes Phineas with a long hug.

Rollie gazes at them intently, and Ito looks at Rollie.

Ryan wakes up in the closet, briefly forgetting where she'd fallen asleep, and rubs her eyes with the palms of her hands. She shakes the blood-flow back into her arm as she exits the closet and opens a bedroom window. Using one hand to shield her eyes from the glinting sun and the other for support on the window ledge, Ryan leans out and sucks in a cleansing breath. A brilliantly red cardinal sings in a cherry-blossom tree with branches so close, its leaves nearly touch the house a few feet to the right of Ryan. The handsome bird holds Ryan in a spell for a few moments, then leaps from its branch and flies away. A smile slowly spreads across Ryan's face before she nods to the morning air and says, "Thank you."

CHAPTER 11

Ito's center is a single-story rectangular building with its name written in traditional Japanese characters on a cedar-shingled awning that spans the building's length. Upon entering, one's eye is drawn to a glittery gold and red tapestry directly across the room that displays a magnificent image of Mount Fuji. Behind the tapestry and several layers of sound-barrier quilts is a door leading to Ito and Ryan's living quarters. When looking to the right of the center's entranceway, one sees four classrooms where Japanese language, music, art, and history are taught. The rest of the space is primarily used for karate, jujutsu, and *takiken* classes. Half of the floor is overlaid with removable mats, and there are several free-standing training dummies along the perimeter. A twenty-five-foot Buddha resides on a wall to the left of the entranceway on the short side of the rectangular space, since the center also doubles as a worship hall. Ito, dressed in a training gi, stands to Ryan's right. Her hair is in two tight braids and she's dressed in shorts, head gear, fingerless gloves, and a protective midriff top. She glistens with sweat as she punches and kicks the air. Standing a few feet from them are Sammy and Bo, two men in their early twenties dressed in head gear, groin guards, and training gloves.

Ito calls out, "Sammy! Bo!" and they advance on Ryan, who slips through them and kicks Sammy in the groin. When he drops to his knees, Ryan spin-kicks him in the head.

Bo jumps on her back and they grapple on the ground.

Ryan puts him in an armbar and he taps out.

Ito jumps in and he and Ryan spar. Ryan's speed and agility are equal to his until she stuns him with a strike to the chin followed by a kick, which he blocks then flips backwards.

Ito commands, *"Supā dake!"* (Spar alone!)

Ryan punches, kicks, spins, flips, and twists with uncanny speed.

Ito shouts, *"Ashita no junbi wa deki teru?"* (Are you ready for tomorrow?)

"Watashi!" (I am!) Droplets of sweat spray from her face as she moves through combinations.

"Dono kurai torēningu shimashita ka?" (How long have you trained?)

"Watashi no isshō!" (My whole life!)

"Darekaga motto isshōkenmei kunren shita koto ga arimasu ka?" (Has anyone ever trained harder?)

"Bangō." (No!)

Ito claps. *"Furoarūchin."* (Floor routine!)

Ryan runs onto the mats and does a gymnastic flipping sequence. After she nails the landing, she goes into deep floor stretches.

Ito points to his forehead. *"Koko de junbi wa īdesu ka?"* (Are you ready here?)

"Watashi!" (I am!)

"Anatahadare?" (Who are you?)

"Shijō saikō no yakyū bōru senshu." (The greatest baseball

ballplayer of all time.)

Ito bows and walks away.

Ryan does a slow-motion press handstand into a one-arm handstand.

Bo and Sammy bow and leave.

Ryan remains on her one arm. Her elegant mid-air pose is as graceful as ballet. Her sculpted muscles resembling the smooth, carved marble of an ancient masterpiece.

CHAPTER 12

Ryan's room is neat, but crammed with the few pieces of furniture necessary for functionality. There's a futon, chest of drawers, and a paper-paneled tower lamp with a bamboo frame that stands across from a small closet and bathroom. Ryan sits on her futon, dressed in baseball pants and a T-shirt, while slowly turning the pages of a large scrapbook. Her tight braid creates a dampened spot on her shirt at the center of her back. The book has pictures of Ryan at various ages and locations with both Japanese and Hispanic ball players. Other photos are of her with Phineas, Rollie, Ito, and international superstar Ichiro Suzuki. She closes the book, places it on top of the dresser, and touches Phineas' photo, which is next to the cottage urn. The urn has a thin, wavy line of smoke streaming from the chimney. Ryan grabs Phineas' old Hounds cap off of a wall hook and exits the room.

Ito walks with Ryan, who totes a backpack stuffed with two bats sticking up in the shape of a V. They walk toward a canopy, behind which is Greyhound Stadium.

Ito looks at Ryan and points to his forehead. "Are you ready here?"

"I am… Like Yogi says, 'baseball is 90% mental. The other half is physical.'"

"I'm glad you brought your sense of humor today."

Ryan smiles and says, "It's so weird, Ito. I've envisioned this day for my entire life. I've walked this path, seen it all so vividly in my mind, yet it doesn't feel anything like the dream, especially since I wasn't anxious in it…" Ryan looks up. "It was also sunnier."

Ito smiles back at her. "The reality is usually different than the fantasies we create, since the future is a mere figment of the imagination."

"In my dreams, Daddy told me how he thought of this moment his whole life. He had this look in his eyes… and he said he was proud of me. I wanted so much to make him proud, and now he's gone and I'll never get to hear him say those words."

"Just because someone is no longer on the physical plane, it doesn't mean you can't hear them."

Ryan looks away, but her focus is pulled toward a group of prospects who attempt, unsuccessfully, to beat her to the registration canopy. A potbellied old-timer wearing a gray shirt with "Greyhounds" written in red script is seated there writing on a chart. He pops a dot onto the paper and looks up at Ryan. "Ma'am, this is a tryout for the LA Greyhounds."

Ryan responds, "I've come to the right place, then."

The prospects look at each other and snigger.

Tree Willis, a tall, strong, inner-city kid in his early twenties wearing a Greyhounds uniform, studies Ryan from the field's entrance gate. Ryan, however, is engaged in the registration process. Tree Willis and Ito stare at each other for a few moments until the youth walks away.

The old timer says, "There are no females in the MLB."

Ryan replies, "There'll be one soon enough."

One of the prospects, dressed as the baseball stereotype right down to the upside-down sunglasses on his cap's visor, busts out laughing.

When Ryan looks at him, he coughs into the crook of his arm.

When she turns away, both he and the rest of his group guffaw.

Ryan focuses on the old-timer. "This is an open tryout, is it not?"

The geezer nods.

"Well… I'm trying out."

He rolls his sleepy eyes and asks, "Name?"

"Ryan Stone."

Inside the park, Tree Willis talks to Rollie in the bullpen located beyond the right field wall. A stocky man in his seventies wearing a Greyhounds uniform and holding a clipboard speed-steps by.

Rollie calls out, "Hey, Chess."

The man turns back. "What's up?"

"We're gonna mix things up today."

Ryan and Ito walk down the third-base line toward the infield. There are groups of prospects scattered around, tossing balls, or talking in cliques.

A voice shouts, "I hope she remembered her cup."

A squall of laughter sets off a string of more jibes and more chortling.

Ito looks at Ryan, who continues walking her path to a group that's gathering near home plate.

An hour later, Tree Willis is on the mound tossing blistering right-handed pitches as Chess talks to a group of approximately fifty prospects clustered near the visitor's dugout. The candidates have paper numbers on their backs. Ryan, #34, stretches in place while listening to Chess. Ito stands thirty feet away with a few other chaperones.

Chess talks to the group with a paternal tone. "We're changing things up today. Y'all will face our top prospect, Tree Willis. You get five swings to show us your stuff."

A man with a goatee near the backstop, holding a clipboard, looks over the group and stops cold when he sees Ryan. Quin Dempsey, twenty-five, is a handsome Boston townie wearing an Under Armour cap and matching pullover that showcases thick chest and arm muscles.

Ryan feels Quin's stare and glances at him.

Quin smiles when their eyes meet, but Ryan turns her attention back to Chess. A few moments later, Ryan gives Quin a furtive once-over while she stretches in place.

Chess adjusts his cup and says, "All pitchers can now make their way to the pens yonder." He points to the bullpens. "Position players should remain here." Chess looks at the pitchers walking away and claps his hands. "Let's see some hustle, boys." They jog toward the outfield and Chess focuses back on the remaining players. "When I call—"

Ryan raises her hand.

"Yes, miss?"

"I'm a position player and a pitcher."

Soft pockets of laughter bounce around.

Chess says, "After your swings, go to the pens." He focuses back on the group, "When I call your name, you'll get a bat near that man, yonder." Quin raises a finger. "…And no… you can't use your lucky bat today…" He looks at his clipboard. "Rick Pap, Ryan Stone, and Gary Perez, you're the first three. The rest of you boys should pay attention to what Tree's throwing." Ryan and the two other prospects, one of whom is Rick Pap – the 'comedian' jock from the registration line – jog toward Quin who stands near the backstop.

Quin tightens his pectorals and checks out Ryan as she searches for a bat. "Let me guess... 32 oz."

Ryan gives Quin a quick glance, then continues searching. "If you get fired here, you can be a fortune teller." She grabs a 32 oz. bat and Quin smiles.

Ito, observing the interaction, makes his way over.

Rick Pap steps into the box and digs in.

Tree winds up and throws heat inside.

Quin asks, "Where've you played?"

Ryan, concentrating on Tree, says, "All over."

Rick Pap swings and Quin jots a note. "I've been scouting for over five years and I ain't never seen you."

Ryan, still eying Tree, says, "Maybe you missed me."

Quin laughs and Ryan looks at him. "I don't think so. I'd remember *you*... It's Ryan, right?"

Ryan's attention is back on Tree, but she gives Quin a slight nod.

"I'm Quin, by the way."

Rick swings, misses again, and walks away frustrated.

"Good luck, Ryan... and watch the inside pitch."

Ryan gives Quin a quick glance as she walks away. "I have eyes."

Quin says, out of Ryan's earshot, "Do you ever!"

Ryan slides on a helmet and looks back at Quin, who smiles at her and then snaps his head to the right when he notices Ito standing beside him.

Ito shouts, *"Anatahadare?"* (Who are you?)

Ryan answers, *"Shijō saikō no yakyū bōru senshu."* (The greatest baseball ballplayer of all time.)

Quin looks at Ito and smiles.

Ito ignores him, as he is fixed on Ryan settling into the box.

Ryan digs in and rocks to-and-fro, her eyes locked on Tree, who wiggles his fingers, winds up, and hurls. The pitch nearly hits her. Ryan whispers, "It's gonna take more than that, big guy."

Ito suddenly takes his eyes off Ryan and scans the park. He freezes when he spots Rollie looking at Ryan with field glasses from the bullpen. Panicked, Ito looks at Tree and then at Ryan. Tree releases a pitch and Ito's eyes pop. The ball cuts inside and crushes Ryan's left elbow.

Ito runs to Ryan, who has dropped to one knee. Her eyes are pinched tight together as she grunts through gritted teeth.

Ito asks, "What are you feeling?"

Ryan's voice is barely audible. "I can't open my fist."

Quin shouts to Chess, "Call an ambulance."

Ryan looks at Quin. "No!"

Quin addresses the gathering prospects. "If I see a cell phone, I shut this down." He then says quietly to Ito, "I heard a crack."

Ryan picks up the bat with her right hand.

Chess comes over with an icepack.

Quin grabs it and asks Ryan, "Can I wrap this around your elbow?"

Ryan nods.

Ito makes a move toward Tree, who's talking to the catcher on the mound. When Tree sees Ito advancing, he flips off his glove.

Ito says, "Tell Rollie I know it was him, you piece of shit."

"Screw you, grandpa."

A siren blares as the catcher gets between Ito and Tree, but Ito turns back to Ryan just as an ambulance pulls up.

Ryan says, "I'm not getting in there, Ito."

"If you choose to remain here with that injury, it could change the course of your life, and you need to choose, now."

Ryan turns away for a beat, grimace, then walks briskly toward the ambulance.

Quin offers her a hand, but she leaps through the open doors – her paper number detaches and falls to the ground. Ito climbs in after her.

Quin looks at Chess with a scrunched brow. "If a major leaguer took it in the elbow like that, he'd be on a stretcher... Who the hell is this girl?" Quin swipes her number off the dirt, looks at it, and calls out, "Hey, Tree... Come over here."

CHAPTER 13

Ryan and Ito walk in silence across the cultural center after business hours. Ryan has a long-arm cast in a sling, her braid is frizzed, and her voice is raspy. "I'll be twenty years old in three months and the plan is nineteen." Her open palm accentuates each word as it's spoken. "Secrecy... MLB at nineteen... Best Ever!"

Ryan and Ito slip behind the Mount Fuji tapestry, past the layers of hanging sound barriers, and into the door of the kitchenette where Ito and Phineas sat forty years prior. It still has the old black stove, wooden cabinets, and the little statues on the window ledge.

Ito lights the burner with a match and places a black kyusu teapot on the grate. "The doctor said it would take four months before you can play. If you can't do it by nineteen, you can't."

Ryan, pacing, raises her gravelly voice. "There is no *can't!*" Her voice cracks on the word 'can't.' "Daddy always said there is no *can't*, and he's not here... He's not here, Ito... to tell me what to do... I need him to tell me what to do! To say it's okay." Ryan rubs the center of her forehead in a circular motion.

Ito calmly fills teacups on the table and looks at Ryan. "You lost your father a week ago and you went out there today to honor him. You shouldn't even be standing up after all you've been through, but here you are, and that, Ryan, is why you're going to win." He kneels on his chabudai cushion and continues, "Do you know what your father did when he encountered bumps in the road? He crushed them. All four foot-five inches of him – an orphan, abused, homeless... He leveled them all."

Ryan, pacing again, says, "That's what I have to do!"

Ito sips his tea. "But now is not the time for action. Stress happens when one tries to solve problems with emotion. And attempting to undo the past turns one into a dog chasing its tail. Silence your mind, listen to your breath, and the answers will find you."

Ryan stands in place for a few beats then looks at Ito serenely sipping his tea. She kneels on her cushion, lifts her cup, and breathes in the steaming liquid with closed eyes.

Ito looks across at Ryan, and smiles.

CHAPTER 14

Ryan jogs along a trail in the San Bernardino Mountains before dawn. Snow blankets the terrain and her smoky breath puffs like a locomotive. She wears a knit hat and hoodie, lugs a large backpack, and her left arm is fettered to her side in a full cast. Ryan thinks about the past.

She is seven years old and stands with clenched teeth holding two rocks on a hot day near a wooded area in Japan. Gnats and other biting insects buzz about and stick to her sweaty face. Her arms and head quiver with greater and greater tremors until she gives way and the rocks drop to the ground.

Ito stares at a stopwatch and says, "Anata ga shippaishita!" (You failed!)

Ryan pleads, "Mōichido yarinaoshimashou!" (Let me try again!)

Ito walks toward the woods and Ryan follows him.

She shouts, "Dekimasu! I can do it!"

Ito continues walking away.

Ryan is in the long-arm cast on a different morning, and she jogs on another frosty San Bernardino trail.

Rollie observes Ryan at the mansion's baseball field as she whacks a ball right-handed on a swing-trainer. The ball rips around, she switches hands and whacks it lefty, then righty, and then lefty again. She repeats this process of hitting, switching sides, and smacking the ball with enigmatic accuracy and power. She is laser focused, oblivious to everything except the zone. She doesn't even hear Rollie's encouragement.

"That's it, Ryan! Attagirl!"

Ryan jogs up a steep hill in the snowy San Bernardino Mountains with a smaller, hinged-fracture brace on her arm.

Ryan, eight, is at a lake in Japan standing on a rock with bare feet, sweating and holding two stones.

Ito stares at his stopwatch.

Her body shakes until the stones fall.

Ito says, "Your parents gave you the physical genes, but they cannot endow discipline. You'll not compete against men unless you master your mind. It's the only way you will beat them. Without that, all of this is for nothing. You must develop your mind, Ryan! You must develop your mind!" He walks away.

"But I'm trying! I'm really trying!"

Ito says, "Jūbun ni muzukashī kotode wa arimasen!" (Not hard enough!)

Ryan screams while thrashing a delicate, flowery bush with a stick. She swings the stick like a bat. Every slice propels flowers into the air. "I hate you, Ito! I hate you so much!"

Ryan jogs in the San Bernardino Mountains, before dawn, saddled with the smaller brace.

Ryan is with Rollie and Ichiro Suzuki at the mansion baseball field. A pitching machine pitches and Ryan, batting left-handed, lays down a bunt and burns a path up the first-base line.

Ichiro says, "That's perfect, Ryan. You were running before your bat touched the ball. That gives you the extra steps needed to increase your chances of a hit, but with your speed I don't think you'll need much of an edge."

Ryan smiles.

Ito looks at Rollie. "I've never seen this kind of speed on an eight-year-old. Can I see that stopwatch?"

Rollie tosses him his stopwatch and Ichiro jogs to first base.

Rollie pats Ryan on the head before she sets herself in the box.

The machine pitches, Ryan bunts toward third base and sprints to first.

Ichiro says, "4.9 seconds."

"That's friggin' lightning." Rollie beams.

Ichiro shakes his head. "I was at 3.7 in the majors. I've never seen anything like this."

"No one has," Rollie tells him.

Ryan looks at Ichiro. "My uncle can be a bit sanguine at times."

Ichiro looks puzzled.

Rollie says, "Sweetie, you need to calm down your vocab so people know what you're talking about."

"Oh, sorry… Overly optimistic."

Ichiro squints his eyes, purses his lips, and moves his head back and forth as he evaluates her statement. "I'm not so sure he is, young lady."

Ryan, free of her arm cast, walks with a flashlight toward a stream running alongside a snowy trail on a sharp, windy morning. She puts the flashlight on the ground, puts her hands on her knees and puffs out thin, frosty vapor before removing a bedsheet from her backpack and submerging it in the icy water. She unzips her hoodie, stuffs it in her tote, and takes a few steps toward the numbing stream, wearing only a swimsuit and hiking boots. She pulls the sheet out of the water, wraps it around her body, grabs the flashlight, and walks, dripping wet, along the blustery terrain to a cliff's edge that juts out over a valley. She unzips her backpack, removes two barbells, and sits in the lotus position beneath a purply sky that's lit by a blizzard of silvery stars while holding the weights straight out over her knees.

On the mansion's patio at night, Ryan trembles as she stands in torrential rain holding two stones.

Ito is fixed on his stopwatch. When the stones drop, he walks away without saying a word. Before entering the building, he looks back and sees the child holding the stones again.

Ryan sits in the lotus position on the cliff's edge with steam rising from the sheet. Her eyes are closed and her arms are as straight as iron rods.

Ryan holds the rocks doggedly as the wind and rain slap and taunt her.

Ito clicks the stopwatch and says, "Seikō." (Success.)

Ryan slowly opens her eyes.

Ito bows to her and she bows to him.

She closes her eyes again and remains holding the stones.

Ryan stands at the mountain's edge as the sun rises. She raises the weights straight up before the horizon's fiery streaks. The sheet slides off and drops to the ground, dry.

CHAPTER 15

*P*hineas sits at the head of the rectangular table in the mansion's conference room. Ito and Kim are seated to his right and Rollie sits across from them on his left.

Phineas hands Rollie an envelope. "This is a severance package. Your services have been invaluable."

Rollie's mouth and brow twist in disbelief. "What the hell?"

"Besides trying desperately to take control of Ryan, you've been stealing from our charity."

"Stealing? That's a crock of shit, Phin! I have every intention of paying it back."

"Two hundred fifty-three thousand dollars? ...Really? ...We could've been arrested. And what about Ryan? Did you think about her?"

"What does Ryan have to do with this?"

"Everything has to do with Ryan."

"I've given my life to Ryan! I gave up my job with the Hounds to mold her into the player she's become."

"While that may be true, let's not forget about the generous signing bonus you received to pay off your loan sharks."

"Listen to me, you little shit. Not you or no one else in this room throws me out." Rollie tosses the envelope on the table. "I'll tell the *world about Ryan… That's right, little man."*

"And I'll tell the world that you've been filching from disabled children to pay off gambling debts."

Rollie's upper lip tightens, exposing his teeth.

Phineas, unfazed, says, "Ito will see you out."

Rollie shoots up and Ito springs to Phineas' side.

Rollie stops, swipes the severance pay off the table, and walks to the door. He turns back toward Phineas. "I'll get you for this!"

Kim Biles starts to talk but Phineas gently touches her hand and says, "You need help, Rollie. Get it."

Rollie spits and walks out, followed by Ito.

Ito and Ryan sit in a sushi restaurant eating with chopsticks.

Ryan says, "I thought Uncle Rollie got fired because he took me on that five-day tournament in Cooperstown while you and Daddy were away… and because he slipped me junk food when no one was watching. I've always felt responsible for his banishment."

"It wasn't anything you did or the junk food – which your father knew about, by the way – it was Rollie's nefarious activities, notwithstanding his growing possessiveness of you. Bringing you to that tournament, however, was the last straw. Rollie cursed and threatened your father the whole time I walked him out the door that day. Phineas thought it was all bluff, but I wasn't convinced of that."

"I can never forgive him, and I have every reason to hate him for what he's done to me, but what I don't understand is *why* he hates me. I just don't get it."

"Rollie loves you, Ryan. You were the light of his life."

Ryan looks confused.

"When some parents get divorced," Ito continues, "they use their children as weapons to hurt their ex. They love their children, but they are blinded by fury."

"That's so awful."

"Yes, it is. Harboring emotions like hatred and being unable to forgive is destructive. You can never be whole unless you free yourself of these."

"Well, Uncle Rollie better hope I don't show up at his door one day. That would not be pretty."

"Ryan, I think you—"

A waiter looks at Ito and shifts his eyes to the right.

Ito slaps down a bill and he and Ryan move in the indicated direction. They stop at the table of Nelson Hernandez, who is now in his mid-forties and the principal owner of the LA Greyhounds. He's a mesomorph poured into an Armani suit.

Nelson looks up. "Hi... It's Ito... right?"

"Yes."

"I'm so very sorry about Phin. I'd have come to the services, but... I was... out of town, and... Who is this young lady?"

"I'm Ryan Stone."

Nelson looks at Ito and then back to Ryan, whose hand is extended.

Ryan says, "It's an honor to meet the owner of the Hounds and the man who hit four home runs in one World Series game."

Nelson smiles. "That's quite a grip, young lady. Please sit."

Ito talks freely to Nelson. Every now and again, Ito uses a hand gesture to make a point, and from time to time, Nelson looks at Ryan, who sits as rigid as a Navy SEAL.

Ito finishes his pitch with, "I'll call Ichiro Suzuki."

"That won't be necessary." Nelson takes out his cell,

punches a few keys, and waits… He eyes Ryan for a beat and then his concentration shifts. "Ichi! Hey, man… Yeah, I'm doing great. You? Good. Good. Hey, I'm here with Ito…" He covers the receiver and looks at Ito.

Ito answers, "Hachi."

Nelson continues, "Ito Hachi and Ryan Stone… That's right, Ryan Stone."

LA Hounds manager Brick Jackson is in his early fifties and wider than he was in his catching days. He looks at a plate of food on his desk and says, "The food *sucks* at this stadium!" as he chucks the plate in the trash. His cramped office contains a file cabinet, a whiteboard, two folding chairs, a closet, and a water cooler standing next to a table housing a microwave and a Keurig coffee machine. Brick is sitting at his desk, which holds a copy of the *LA Times* with the following headline – *Brick Jackson Tossed Again As Hounds Lose 11th straight. Private practice scheduled today.* The photo beneath the headline is of Brick with popped eyeballs and his finger pointed in an umpire's face.

Brick's cell buzzes and he unsnaps his belt case and pulls it out.

He looks at it and shakes his head before he taps the screen and says, "Hey, chief… I can't right now. I have a team meeting in – Hello? Nellie? That son of a…" He clicks off his phone and opens his office door. "If anyone leaves before I get back, I'll fine yo' ass!"

The pitching-cage area of Greyhound Stadium is an underground, windowless room housing a configuration of rectangular cages constructed of chain-link fencing. Each cage – some vertical, others horizontal – is the approximate length of the pitching mound to home plate. Behind home plate is a shock-absorbing blanket that prevents missed pitches from ricocheting around the cage.

Ito and Nelson stand in the entrance gate of one such cage. Ryan is on the mound and Nelson holds a radar gun.

Nelson says, enthusiastically, "Fifty-five!" as Brick approaches with an expression akin to one who's inhaled a foul odor.

Brick gives Ito a quick glance before he addresses Nelson. "Mr. Hernandez... sir... how does it look if I call a player meeting and—"

"Hey, Brick, lookie here... Oh, by the way, this is Ito Hachi. Ito, meet Brick Jackson." He calls out to Ryan, standing on the mound inside the cage, "Throw the knuckleball." He turns back to Brick. "Oh, and that's Ryan Stone."

Ryan winds up and throws a ball that moves through the air with the tone-deaf rhythm of an awkward dancer, but then slides through the strike zone of the blanket.

Nelson checks the radar. "Sixty!"

Brick looks at Ryan, then at Nelson, and then Ito. Brick calls out, "Can I see another one like that, young lady?"

Nelson quips, "Somebody's in a better mood."

"Don't gimme dat! We gonna talk later... And you owe me dinner for this!"

Ryan winds up and releases another confused ball that floats and flops into the strike zone.

Brick looks at Nelson. "That's unhittable shit!"

"You ain't seen nothin' yet." Nelson calls out, "Hey, Ryan, throw the fastball."

The ball smacks the blanket and Nelson calls out, "Eighty-eight!" He looks at Brick and says "Hey, Ryan, throw the curve."

Ryan's pitch arcs from ten feet to two feet in the half-second journey to home plate.

Nelson shouts, "Eighty-two... Now the slider."

The ball flies in chest high but drops into the bottom of the zone.

Nelson looks at Brick. "And check this out... Ryan, let's see the screw ball."

Ryan throws that anomalous pitch for a strike.

Brick talks into his cell... "Yeah, Rocky, tell the guys to get on the field." He looks at Nelson. "Let's see her with hitters."

Greyhound Stadium has its executive offices in a ten-story glass building that stretches across the back of the ballpark in the place of traditional seating. The building's placement and curved design turn Greyhound Stadium into a circular arena, since they rent the bottom eight floors of the building for six thousand dollars per game. These luxury suites offer an unobstructed view, chef-prepared meals, flat screens, and an open bar. Fans literally surround the stadium and when they cheer the building doubles as a sound barrier, making it the loudest in all of Major League Baseball.

The top two floors of the structure are the Hounds' executive offices. The interior has artfully placed posters, pennant and world series flags, and Hounds' logos, giving the space an air of history, pride, and positivity. The main hall features comfortable chairs near desks with secretaries and glass-walled offices along both sides. Some offices have a clear view of employees typing, talking on the phone, or conversing in groups, while other rooms are darkened by smoked privacy glass.

Brick, Nelson, Ito, and Ryan, carrying a briefcase, walk together around a bend to an office with *Nelson Hernandez* inscribed on a plaque above the doorway. Outside the office is a secretary talking with a man who is sitting on her desk.

Nelson glances her way and says, "Hold my calls, Sally."

Sally looks up, startled.

Her companion is Quin Dempsey, the Boston townie Ryan met at open tryouts. Quin and Ryan exchange a glance as she walks into Nelson's office. Seconds later, the glass is darkened.

Quin asks, "Will they be long?"

"This wasn't scheduled, so I don't know, but you can stay as long as you like."

Quin talks to the smitten secretary for a while but leaves after thirty minutes. He looks at Nelson's privacy glass a few times as he heads down the corridor.

Nelson's spacious office is located on the ninth floor of the building and has an extraordinary stadium view. Not only is the office positioned in the middle of the stadium, but the floor-to-ceiling glass panels to the left of the room's center, have custom-fitted flatscreen TVs. Nelson has the perfect combination of live-game energy plus slow motion, trivia, interviews, and the rest of the broadcast perks.

Ryan stands opposite Nelson, who sits behind his desk in a large leather chair, behind which is the magnificent backdrop of Greyhound Stadium.

Brick sits to Nelson's right and Ito sits to Ryan's left.

Ryan ends her presentation with, "...Secrecy, MLB at nineteen, best ever. I've lived by that mantra my whole life." She turns to Ito. "May I please have the folder?"

Brick and Nelson look at each other as Ryan places a stapled packet on the desk.

Ryan says, "I'm tendering this contract..."

Nelson asks incredulously, "Contract?"

Brick smirks. "Are you a lawyer, too, young lady?"

"I received my high school diploma at eight years old, I was tutored by professors from Harvard Law, and I have an IQ of one-ninety-seven. I'm more than capable of writing a baseball contract."

Brick retorts, "We are the ones who offer you the contract. That's the way it works, dolly."

Nelson reads from the paper. "If you're injured, you'll donate your salary back to the Greyhounds?"

"Yes, sir. As you read on, you'll see that it's incentive based. I shouldn't be paid if I'm not contributing."

Brick, incensed, growls, "Nellie… You ain't actually considering this horseshit, are you?"

"I've never seen anyone who could throw a fifty MPH knuckleball, an eighty-eight MPH fastball, a wicked curve, a filthy slider, and a screwball, all from different release points. Besides that, I just watched her strike out most of our team, so, yes, she has my attention."

Brick looks at Ryan and then back to Nelson, who is reading the contract. "That wasn't a game, man. For all I know our guys pranked us and are laughing their damn asses off right now!"

Nelson looks at Ryan. "It says here you have to play in a major-league game before your twentieth birthday. May I ask how old you are?"

"I'll be twenty in ten days."

Brick blurts out, "What!"

"If we don't settle this today, Mr. Hernandez, I'm sorry, but I'll never come back… not even in a trade. I can go down the street to the Dodgers, who made history when Branch Rickey signed Jackie Robinson in 1945."

Brick cuts in, "Branch Rickey didn't sign Jackie and put him on the damn field in a week."

Ryan looks at Brick. "Either way, it was a risk, and Mr. Rickey was written into history books."

She turns to Nelson. "Do you want to share that space with Mr. Rickey or be the man who turned down the opportunity to sign the first female major leaguer? Besides, from a financial standpoint, the Hounds will be at the center of the baseball world and that will generate huge team awareness and profits. Branch Rickey understood the tidal wave of signing Mr. Robinson, but he did it anyway. Are you ready for the greatest moment is sports since then? Because I'm going to make history with you or with someone else. It's your choice."

Brick stands up. "Are you strong-armin' Nelson Hernandez?"

Ryan turns to Ito. "Are you ready?"

He nods and they get up and walk away.

Nelson stops them as they approach the door. "Wait."

The smile fades from Brick's face. Brick glares at Nelson "Wait? … Wait? You lost your damn mind, Nellie? You thinkin'-a putting a nineteen-year-old girl in a Greyhounds uniform and having her pitch in a major-league game without a minor-league stint? Not on my watch, you ain't."

"I've made no promises yet, Brick."

"*Yet?* This is bullshit! I'm tellin' you right now, Nellie, I ain't taking the heat if this gets ugly, and it will get ugly. I'm throwing all y'alls under the bus." Brick storms out of the room.

CHAPTER 16

Greyhound Stadium is packed with fans on a gorgeous summer day as they host the first-place cross-state rival San Francisco Waves. Both teams are lined up along the third and first base lines as a tenor from the Los Angeles Fire Department sings "The Star-Spangled Banner."

O say, can you see, by the dawn's early light,

The first line is heard in a tunnel below Hounds Stadium by a shadowy walking figure popping a ball into a glove. Both the popping ball and the metallic sound of cleats against concrete echo in the shaft.

What so proudly we hailed at the twilight's last gleaming,

Ito rushes up a ramp, weaving around other tardy fans. He has a large, rolled canvas under his arm.

Whose broad stripes and bright stars,

The tunnel where the shadowy figure walks grow more illuminated, revealing the back of Ryan's red jersey, with *"STONE"* scripted in gray letters outlined in white above the number *"34"* in the same color combo. She wears a red belt and gray cleats with red socks pulled up to her gray pants, detailed with two thin red stripes down the sides. Her cap is red with a gray bill and an interlocking gray *"LA"* outlined in white on the cap's front panel. The front of her jersey has *"Greyhounds"* in the red-and-white color combo written in script on an upward tilt across her jersey.

Through the perilous fight,

Brick Jackson stands outside the dugout wiping away sweat with a towel.

O'er the ramparts we watched,

Nelson wipes sweat off his brow with a handkerchief as he stands in his office looking out through the glass panels.

Were so gallantly streaming?

Radio personalities Dan Devine and Shelly Shaw stand with hands on their hearts. They are both short and dark-haired, in their fifties, and have such similar facial features they could pass for siblings.

And the rocket's red glare, the bombs bursting in air,

Ito stands with his hand on his heart at the edge of the loge seating located above home plate.

Gave proof through the night that our flag was still there.

Ryan sees blazing, white sunlight at the end of the tunnel as she steps closer.

Oh, say, does that star-spangled banner yet wave,

Dozens of reporters take videos and stills of the singer.

O'er the land of the free and the home of the brave?

The players and umps scatter to their positions.

Ryan enters the dugout and sees Brick waving her onto the field.

"C'mon woman… Let's go. Let the circus begin." After Ryan passes him, Brick says to himself, "I don't beleed' d-shit!"

Ryan jogs out to the mound and the visiting team bunches up in the dugout, staring…

Waves manger Gil Tod, a white-haired man in his late sixties, looks at his bench coach and then back at Ryan, who puts her foot on the rubber.

Gil asks, "Is there a ceremonial pitch today?"

Ryan turns away from Gil and he sees the back of her jersey. He does a double take and points at his roster card. "*That's* Ryan Stone?"

Rollie is sitting in a luxury box one level above Ito, smoking. He stares at Ryan through binoculars then grabs his cell and taps the pad. "You said her elbow was shattered... Yeah, well, put the damn game on!"

Tree Willis sits on the dugout bench next to pitcher Benny Gross, who's holding a bag of sunflower seeds.

Tree elbows Benny. "Did you hear that I broke her elbow at open tryouts?"

Benny spits out a shell. "And they promoted you?"

"I guess they thought I had good aim." Tree laughs.

Benny smiles. "I never know when you're joking... Wait. You ain't serious, right?"

In the radio booth, Shelly Shaw picks through some papers as Dan Devine speaks into a desk mic.

"Her name is Ryan Stone and that's all we know. Oh, and she's a pitcher."

Ito stands at the edge of the balcony and pours a small canister of Phineas' ashes into the center of the rolled canvas.

Brick, Gil, and an umpire are gathered at home plate.

Gil asks, "A high-school girl's your pitcher? Is this a joke?"

"Are you saying girls are inferior?"

"I never said that, Brick!"

"Well then, maybe it's discrimination. You know I can go on like this all damn-day."

BORN FOR THE GAME

The umpire interrupts. "Protest it if you want, Gil, but we have a baseball game to play."

Ito blasts an airhorn before unfurling the rolled canvas into a gust of wind. Phineas' ashes swirl and dissipate into the stadium air. The canvas has the LA Hounds logo.

Ryan looks up and smiles as the ump shouts, "Play ball!"

Willy Stubbs, a short right fielder, is in the on-deck circle.

Gil Tod approaches him. "Introduce her to the big leagues, Willy."

Willy walks to the batter's box, looks at Javy, and says with a smirk, "This is gonna be fun."

Ryan opens her locket, kisses it, clicks it closed, and tucks it back into her jersey. She pulls her visor down, winds up fast, and releases a slow knuckle ball.

Willy swings, misses, and nearly falls over.

There's a mixture of laughter and cheers from the rambunctious crowd.

Javy chuckles and says, "Not so funny now… is it, bruh?"

Dan Devine talks into the mic. "And she's in the books, Shelly. The first female in the history of Major League Baseball has thrown a first-pitch strike."

Shelly says, "And how! That was a nasty knuckleball."

Rollie grimaces when he sees Ito watching the game a level below him.

Willy Stubbs readies himself for the next pitch. He spits and waggles the bat above his head like it's some kind of conductor. There's no crowd, no Javy, no ump – it's just him and Ryan. As the bat orbits above his head, he studies her every movement – her eyes, her body language, her breath.

Ryan gets the call from Javy, winds up, and releases a high fastball, which explodes on Willy in a flash.

He swings hard and pops it straight up.

Javy tosses his mask, carefully places himself under the ball, and holds out his glove, as nonchalantly as if he were waiting for a cashier to return change. The ball plops into Javy's glove and the fans roar and taunt Willy on his long walk back to the visitor's dugout.

Dan Devine shouts, "She backed up that knuckler with an eighty-eight MPH fastball."

Shelly adds, "Ooh! She's got some spunk in her, too. That was dirty! I mean, you really can't blame Willy. There are very few players who'd be able to handle those two pitches back-to-back."

The next batter digs in and Ryan throws a high-diving curve that freezes him. The fans' cheers bounce off the Hounds' offices and ricochet around the stadium. The ump shouts, "Steeerike!"

"That curve was unhittable, Dan. She is the real deal, and I think the Waves know it!"

Ryan's next pitch is a knuckleball.

The batter takes an awkward swing and the ump reacts with a louder and more exaggerated, "Twoooo!"

The pumped fans scream as Ryan peers in, winds up slowly, and fires a fastball up in the zone.

The ball blows past the batter and the ump twists to his right, drops on one knee, punches his arm straight out, and roars like a pirate, "You're arrr!"

The batter walks away shaking his head to the screams and insults of the psyched crowd.

"Oh! What a stunning array of pitches! I am astounded, Shelly!"

The third Waves' batter pushes through the palpable cheers as he walks to the box and sets himself.

Ryan peers in, winds up, pushes her foot off the rubber,

and tosses a slow knuckleball.

The batter swings hard and hits a lazy flyball to centerfielder Johnny Oaks, a strong, good-looking young player with bleached-blond hair, tattoos, and rock-star swagger.

Oaks catches it with ease and the Hounds jog in to a standing ovation.

Ryan is greeted with high-fives by her teammates, but Johnny Oaks ignores her and sits next to Tree Willis and Benny Gross at the north end of the bench.

Brick notices the slight just before Ryan passes him. He says, "Good inning, Ryan," before shooting daggers at Tree, Benny, and Oaks.

Oaks notices Brick in his peripheral vision and turns toward him.

Brick looks at his brazen centerfielder long enough to send a message before he turns his attention back to the game. He claps his hands. "All right, let's get Ryan some runs, now."

Ryan continues through the game by baffling the Waves with pitch sequences they've never experienced before. While she mostly throws her funky knuckleball, batters must also deal with an abundance of trickery. At times she winds up fast and throws a slow floater. Other times it's the reverse order. Sometimes it's a fast wind up and fast pitch or a slow wind up and a slow pitch. She also changes arm angles, which gives the same pitch a different look. Another aspect adding to the Waves' frustration is the unspoken gender-role expectations embedded in their psyche. Phrases such as, *"You swing like a girl,"* or, *"You throw like a girl,"* are the subconscious taunts fueling the Waves, the Hounds, the media, and the crowd.

Ryan gets her first at bat in the third inning. A buzz pulses through her body as she walks up to the plate. The first pitch nearly hits her and the crowd boos. Ryan expected that one as both a formal introduction to the big leagues and in retaliation for making them look so bad. She thinks, however, that they can't push it further because they would be bashed by the media if they hit her. She gets back in the box and readies herself for the next pitch, which comes in hard, but covers more of the plate. She sticks her bat out and lays down a bunt single.

Shelly Shaw is standing. "That was Ichiro-esque, and has she ever got some wheels on her! I'll bet she was up the line in under four seconds!"

Ito cheers.

Nelson swings a bat in his office box.

Brick claps from the lip of the dugout.

Gil Tod turns to curse at the dugout wall.

The cheerful voice of Dan Devine rings over the air waves. "It's zero-to-zero in the fifth, but the bigger story is that Ryan Stone, the first female in the bigs, is perfect thus far. It's been fifteen up and fifteen down, and twelve of them have been strikeouts!"

Shelly jumps in, "Oh, and that last pitch had fangs. Good God, she is amazing!"

Rollie, clenching a cigarette between his teeth, is in the stadium bathroom drying his hands under an air blower. He is approached by a man in his forties holding a Sharpie and gesturing to his seven-year-old son.

The father asks, "Mr. Rollins, would you be kind enough to sign my son's shirt?"

The boy holds out his arm. His beaming grin reveals a gap of two missing front teeth.

Rollie walks past them without looking. "Why? So you

could sell it on eBay?" He walks out the door, leaving the gap-toothed boy still grinning and his father with his pen in the air.

Johnny Oaks swings and crushes a monster home run.

"Did Oaksie ever get all of that one! That had to be over four hundred feet."

Shelly joins in, "And that puts the Hounds on the scoreboard."

Javy ropes a double up the middle, which leaves him standing on second base with Ryan coming to bat.

Ryan fouls off the first two pitches then rips a single between first and second.

"That's her second hit of the game, and give her an RBI to boot!" Shelly says.

Ryan takes a generous lead off of first base. The Waves' pitcher throws over, but Ryan dives back in time. She dusts off her uniform, takes a few strides toward second, and then a few more sideways steps, keeping her eyes fixed on the pitcher. The moment he commits to pitch, she bolts toward second and slides in before the tag.

"That was a textbook steal and slide. They had no chance. Absolutely no chance. This is utterly amazing, Shell!"

"It is, Dan, and the fans are eating it up. They haven't sat down since the first inning. Ladies and gentlemen, it is electric at Greyhound Stadium today!"

The eighth inning scoreboard shows: Hounds 2 - Waves 0. Footage of the scoreboard is being broadcast live around the country. People watch from TVs at home, at bars, and on the other side of the country in Times Square. People are talking about it, tweeting about it, and analyzing it on the radio. The whole country is obsessed with what's happening in this previously insignificant game between the last-place LA Hounds and their first-place cross-state rivals.

"And she ends her eighth perfect inning with her sixteenth strikeout! How was I to know that when I got up this morning, I'd be announcing the most exciting game of my career?"

"Your career?" asks Shelly "Ever! There's a woman in the majors who may pitch a perfect game in her debut, and she's three-for-three at the plate with a stolen base."

Brick talks to Ryan on the bench. "You good, Ryan?"

"I'm great, Mr. Jackson."

"The last inning is just an inning. Just get three. That's it." He uses exaggerated hand gestures while he speaks. "Easy, right? It's just like any other inning. Don't think about the perfect game, okay?"

"I won't, sir. I'm just playing catch with Javy."

"Yeah, that's the attitude, girl. You got this! Don't think about it. I'm not, so why should you?"

Ryan smiles, grabs her glove, and trots to the mound.

An angry Waves player nicknamed "The Beard" due to his twelve inches of unruly facial hair, steps in and whacks Ryan's first pitch up the middle.

Val Sando, a veteran player, dives, grabs it in the hole, throws to first on his knees, and nabs him.

"Oh my!" Shelly exclaims. "Sando hasn't made a play like that in ten years. She's ignited this whole team."

"She certainly has, Shelly. How much fun is this?"

The next batter hits a foul ball toward the seats, but Abnar Cruz, the Hound's first baseman, leans into the stands, catches it, and takes a nacho from a fan's plate. The Stadium, which became filled to capacity over the course of the game, has every fan, concessions worker, custodian, and anyone else in the ballpark standing and cheering.

"That's two pitches, two outs, one less nacho for a fan, and number twenty-seven is up at bat for the final out of a game that will go down in history."

Shelly adds, "The only thing between Ryan Stone and baseball immortality is the deadly pinch hitter El Caballo. My God! I can hardly hear myself talk it's so loud right now."

El Caballo has a wide chin-strap beard, stands six foot five, and weighs in at two hundred seventy-five pounds. He stares at Ryan the way an angry street fighter does in the moments before the first punches fly. El Caballo slams the donut off his bat, walks with heavy steps to the batter's box and sets himself, still glaring, still fixed on Ryan.

Ito is at the edge of the seating rail.

Rollie smokes.

Nelson paces.

Both teams stand to cheer on their respective teammate.

Ryan throws a knuckleball strike, which El Caballo takes looking. The next knuckleball is outside.

Javy lays down the fastball sign and taps the inside of his thigh.

Ryan shakes off the pitch and Javy calls for a screwball. Ryan nods, winds up, and deals.

El Caballo swings powerfully and his bat splinters.

The ball arcs slowly over Ryan's head as the bat's barrel shoots up the mound. Ryan leaps as the jagged wood grazes her spikes.

Sando charges the ball from second base.

Ryan lands on the mound as the ball is passing overhead. She leaps high, nabs it with an outstretched arm, and the momentum causes her to backflip. As her feet are about to touch the ground, Sando slams into her like a linebacker surprising a quarterback. Ryan is propelled forward and smacks the ground face-first, but she clamps onto the ball and holds it in the air.

The ump screams, "You're out!" and the stadium explodes in cheers.

Dan Devine's velvety radio voice is reduced to that of a boy in the throes of puberty. "Holy cow! That's the single greatest catch I've ever seen. Who is she? Where does she come from, and how did she get here?"

Shelly shouts, "The first female pitcher in MLB history to touch a baseball has just pitched a perfect game! Ladies... Oh, was it ever worth the wait!"

Javy picks Ryan up and carries her around.

Nelson pops a bottle of Prosecco.

Fans hug each other.

Ito waves his banner.

Dan Devine grips the mic. "She's the first woman to play in the majors and the first player to ever pitch a perfect game in a debut. Those records are hers forever."

Javy and Sando furtively carry a barrel of Swiftwater Fuel while Ryan is being interviewed, and they baptize her on live TV. She cringes as she pulls the jersey from her pants and ice cubes plop out. Javy and Sando laugh and point at her as they run back to the dugout.

Nelson sits across from Dan Devine in the radio booth. "Yeah, we planned it that way. She's one of a kind and I wanted her debut to be worthy of that."

Gil Tod is being interviewed by a reporter in the visitors' locker room. "That's exactly what I'm saying! There's bad blood between us and, with interleague over, we won't meet again, unless by some miracle the Hounds make it to the World Series. It was unprofessional to put a pitcher on the mound who is basically a ghost."

Ryan and Brick are surrounded by a sea of reporters in the locker room.

Brick leans into the bed of microphones. "Oh yeah, I knew she was special the moment I saw her."

A reporter calls out from the crowd, "Ms. Stone, where'd you train?"

"Mostly in Japan and Cuba."

A Latina reporter asks, "*¿Eres fluida en español?*" (Are you fluent in Spanish?)

Ryan answers, *"Soy fluida en italiano, español, y japonés."* And then interprets, "I'm fluent in Italian, Spanish, and Japanese."

Another reporter asks, "How did you get to Cuba?"

Ryan points to Ito, standing a few feet away. "My father and I are dual US/Japanese citizens, so we traveled to Cuba via Japan."

Several reporters detach from the crowd and surround Ito.

As Tree Willis, Johnny Oaks, and Benny Gross are about to leave the stadium, a reporter approaches them with an outstretched mic.

Oaks says, "We're just headin' out but I have a minute. Yeah... I knew he was gonna throw the curve so I waited and crushed it."

The reporter replies, "Great! Do you know what size bat Ryan uses or where her locker is?"

"What do I look like, an equipment manager? Take a hike, asshole."

Ryan, Brick, Ito, Nelson, and Javy are in the locker room as Brick escorts the reporters out.

Javy looks at Ryan. "I'm gonna shower and then we're heading out, okay?"

Ryan nods and Javy leaves.

Nelson shakes her hand. "You made your father proud tonight..."

"Thank you, Mr. Hernandez."

Nelson smiles. "Damn, you got some grip, kid!"

He then walks away, leaving Ryan and Ito alone.

"The guys invited me out... Do you mind?"

"The moment you stepped onto that field you were on your own. That's always been the plan."

Ryan looks at Ito for a beat. "I have no words."

Ito smiles and bows.

Ryan bows and hurries away. She waves before disappearing around a corner.

Rollie drives on the freeway, smoking and talking into his cell. "I got a new plan, and it's genius."

CHAPTER 17

Bobby Ray's Restaurant is popular among society's elite, as its steely bouncers both guard the entrance and select the clientele. The food is terrible and offensively expensive, but the rich and famous can hobnob there without predator paparazzi, starstruck fans, or obsessed psychopaths.

While the eatery begins heating up after 11:00 pm, Bobby Ray opens his doors early to accommodate the local pro teams who play afternoon games. After Ryan's dismantling of the Waves, her teammates are drinking together around a long, rectangular table in the relatively empty restaurant: Ike Green, Felix Mendoza, Pete O'Neill, Ray White, and Sammy Buckets – a moniker Sammy earned because he walks in a rocking manner as though he's carrying buckets in his balled-up fists.

Tree Willis, Johnny Oaks, and Benny Gross sit together at a bar twenty feet behind their teammates. They bite into salted lime wedges, down shots of Patron, slap their glasses onto the bar, and shiver through the burn.

Tree says, "Just wait 'til everyone gets the video on her. It'll be lights out. Her fastball tops out at what? …Eighty-five?"

"I think she was hitting eighty-eight consistently."

Tree shoots back, "What difference does it make? Big league hitters will drive anything under ninety MPH into the upper deck."

Ryan, Javy, Sando, and Abnar walk into the restaurant together.

Oaks sees them, elbows Tree, and points to Ryan.

Tree says, "This is such bullshit! Let's bounce." He calls out to the bartender, "Hey, Louie, put it on my tab."

Louie nods and Tree and his group exit past Ryan.

Ryan and Tree look at each other as they pass.

Sando asks, "Do you and Tree have a problem?"

Ryan says, "Not tonight."

Javy smirks. "He's a *pendejo*, anyway."

The Hounds clap as Ryan approaches their table, which has filled Champagne flutes at each setting.

Javy clinks his glass with a butter knife and raises it.

Ryan raises a glass of water.

Javy clears his throat before speaking. "Congrats, Ryan, on your perfect game. And an especially big thanks from me, because now I'll be in the history books, too."

The team says, "To Ryan," before downing their drink.

Ryan says, "Thanks so much, guys. I'm so happy to be here!"

Buckets and O'Neill sit on either side of Ryan.

Buckets leans over. "I've always wanted to throw a knuckleball because it's a perfect change-up. What you're going is genius. Can you teach it to me?"

"And you gotta tell me what you're doing to make your slider drop like that," O'Neill adds.

Ryan says, "Of course... but let me get a seltzer at the bar, first. I'm so dehydrated. I'll be right back." She makes her way to the bar, sits, and motions to the bartender. "May I have a large seltzer with lime?"

Louie winks. "Sign my book and your drinks are on me."

Ryan smiles, signs it, and hands it back. She looks at the TV, and Dakota Swiftwater is holding a bottle of Swiftwater II Liquid Fuel. He says, "Fuel up with zero carbs."

Willy Stubbs, the Waves' leadoff hitter, approaches Ryan from behind. "Next time we'll be ready for you."

Ryan smiles. "Looking forward to it."

Willy runs the back of his fingers along Ryan's neck tattoo. "Does this run all the way down the front—"

Ryan grabs his hand and puts him in a standing armbar. Her teammates rise. Ryan whispers, "I'm not snapping your wrist because you're drunk, but come at me when I let go, and I'll end your season." She holds him tight and twists it farther.

Stubbs says, "Okay! Okay! Let go!" and Ryan pushes him away. Stubbs peers around at the onlookers and then turns toward Ryan. "You're lucky you're a girl, you stupid bitch!" he shouts, before walking away.

Ryan turns and bumps into Quin, who puts his hands up. "Please don't break anything."

Ryan says, "Please don't touch anything."

"Three months ago you had a broken elbow, and today you pitch a perfect game?"

Ryan responds, "I know. I was there."

"Can I buy you a drink?"

Ryan downs her seltzer. "No, thank you."

Quin follows her. "How about dinner?"

"I saw you talking to Mr. Hernandez's secretary last week."

"Sally? …She's a good friend of mine. Hey, how about I

don't buy you anything and we just talk?"

"How about no, and you leave?"

Quin gets closer and looks her in the eyes. "Do you really want me to?"

"You're way too close, and yeah, I really do."

Quin gives her puppy-dog eyes and walks away.

Ryan thinks for a few beats, turns back toward Quin, but stops and takes a hard left into the bathroom. She fans herself, teepees her shirt, and pops it up and down several times. She douses her face with water and dabs herself dry. She looks in the mirror. "Easy, tiger! No boys for one year. It's only a year... I can do this. I can definitely do this." She takes a deep breath, taps her cheeks with open palms, and walks out of the bathroom.

After a few steps, Quin comes up from behind her. "Ryan!"

"Ahh!" Ryan puts her hand on her heart. "You scared the crap out of me." She laughs, then playfully punches him on the arm.

"This is progress. The Titanic chips off a piece of the iceberg." Ryan smirks and Quin continues, "Now, what can I do to win you over?"

Ryan taps her chin. "Hmm... Not really sure, but you *do* know what happened to the Titanic after it hit the iceberg, right?"

Quin's epiphany is followed by a raised index finger. "Ah. Great catch... Okay! Umm... Will begging work?"

Ryan looks around, a little embarrassed. "What?"

"Hey, that is not below me. Wait!" He gets down on one knee. "How's this?" Ryan cocks an eyebrow and Quin says with open palms, "Two knees

CHAPTER 18

Quin's apartment is shaped like a backwards letter L. Walking in, there's a bed straight ahead. To the right of the bed is a chest of drawers and a closet. To the left is a desk and a small table with an open pack of cigarettes, an ash tray, and a lighter. Continuing left beyond the table is a galley kitchen with windows and a patio door. There's a bathroom at the end of the kitchen, and opposite the kitchen is a wall with large windows offering a view of the street.

While Quin may don designer clothes, his living space is representative of his true financial bracket. The furniture looks as though it's older than its resident, having possibly been purchased from a second-hand store or included with the apartment. The room is fairly clean, but it's messy. There are clothes on the bedposts and floor, and there's a pile of dishes in the sink.

Quin picks up clothes as he and Ryan enter. He extends his free arm and gives a quick bow. "My very humble abode…" He shoots a ball of clothes into an open closet. "Hey, would you like a beer, wine, Tito's?"

Ryan grabs the lighter off the table and flicks it on. "I'll take a water if you have one."

"You got it," says Quin as he walks past her.

Ryan checks him out from behind on his way to the fridge. He grabs a bottle of Sam Adams for himself and tosses a water to Ryan, who is standing near the doorway. They each take a slug and smile in an awkward moment of silence.

The combination of Ryan's perfect game, first night of freedom, and pent-up passion flicks some primal switch inside of her.

Quin says, "So—"

Ryan chucks her open water bottle across the room as she walks with verve to Quin and kisses him up against the refrigerator. His beer shatters on the tile floor as they kiss each other into the bed area. Quin flicks off the lights and Ryan breaks away. She catches her breath and says, "Wait. Stay right here."

Ryan goes to the chair by the door and sits.

She grabs a cigarette. "You don't smell like a smoker."

"Those are a friend's." Ryan flicks the lighter, and Quin asks, "Do you smoke?"

"No. I just want to play with it while you strip for me."

"Strip? Right here?"

She brushes on the light switch. "Right here. I want to see this."

"Hmm… I have a much better idea. How about you strip for me?"

Ryan shakes her head slowly. "I guess you're not as interested as I thought."

"I am… very."

Ryan fires up the lighter. "Talk is cheap." She puts a cigarette between her teeth and touches it to the flame.

"Okay." Quin cracks his knuckles and rubs his hands together before he undoes his belt.

As he pulls off his shirt, Ryan takes a long drag on the cigarette, parts her lips, and pushes the smoke out slowly, causing it to slide up her face. She continues this process of pulling in smoke and letting it out slowly until Quin is completely naked. Ryan takes in another mouthful of smoke, then points her index finger straight up and slowly twirls it.

"You want me to turn around?"

Ryan blows the smoke out softly while nodding.

Quin, ungracefully, begins to turn.

Ryan says, "Slower... and be careful you don't knock anything over, now."

Quin chuckles and turns around more slowly. "Better?"

"Much better." When Quin is in profile, she says, "Hold that pose..." Ryan crushes the cigarette in the ashtray and raises an eyebrow. "If I threw a fastball, I believe you may be able to hit a line drive."

"I bet I could hit a home run."

"Really now... Be cognizant of the curve ball."

Sex had not been taboo in Ryan's home, as she'd been given the Kama Sutra and various tantric books in her early teens so she would not be suffocated by religious and societal restraints. Sex was viewed as a private matter, but as natural as sleeping, eating, or breathing.

Ryan flips off her shoes and shirt while rising and then her jeans and underwear go in a quick pull. She unhooks her bra and lets it drop to the floor as she approaches Quin, who responds as though he's seeing a nude woman for the first time. Ryan breathes in Quin's seductive gaze as he walks around her.

He drags two fingers along the path of her tattoos, barely touching her skin. His fingers roll slowly over the smooth bumps of her muscles. Quin says, "You are the most beautiful woman to ever walk this earth."

Ryan reaches behind his head with both hands and kisses him. She pauses for a moment and talks with her lips against his. "At the bar, you said something about... *both* knees." She slides her hands down the back of his neck, laying her fingertips on his large, muscular shoulders. A gentle push down and his knees bend... After a beat, her chin jerks up and she sucks in a quick breath. "You may hit a home run after all."

A few hours later, Ryan and Quin are in bed facing each other, but Ryan's eyes are closed.

Quin touches her locket. "This is beautiful. Where'd you get it?"

Ryan's words are dragging along the edge of slumber. "It was a gift from my father on my thirteenth birthday."

Quin asks, "What's inside?" but Ryan is asleep. Quin twirls the locket in his fingers.

Phineas twirls Ryan's locket and says, "This grows in beauty as you grow more beautiful." He is dressed in a suit and Ryan, nineteen, is in baseball attire at the mansion's field. Behind them is Phineas' red Ferrari. Ryan smiles and Phineas continues his thought, "Which is another reason why you need to stick to the plan." Ryan bites the side of her cheek and Phineas says matter-of-factly, "No boys until you go pro. They'll complicate things... And even after you turn pro, you shouldn't date anyone for at least a year. You've waited too long for this, and guys will complicate your life at a time when you are adjusting to a world in which you're not accustomed... And you cannot trust them."

"You're a guy."

"Exactly!"

Ryan asks, "Is this about Rafael?"

"About your recent Cuba trip, yes, and it's also about Hideki in

Japan."

"Ito needs to stay out of my business. I'm nineteen years old."

"I know you are, and we are almost there, my dear. The rules have gotten us this far, right? And, trust me, in a year, you'll have so many boys, you won't even remember this talk... or their names, for that matter." He smiles.

Ryan gives a slight shrug and jogs toward home plate. "Hey, Daddy, I want to show you something." She grabs a bat, slaps on a helmet, then presses a button that awakens a pitching machine. Gears spin, lights flash, and it spits out an angry fastball. Ryan takes a hack, but whiffs. She puts up an index finger then refocuses on the machine. It slings another bullet and Ryan foul tips it.

Phineas looks at his watch. "Honey, I'm going to miss my flight."

"One sec." Ryan crushes the next ball, sending it twenty feet over the fence. She clicks the machine off and jogs back to Phineas. She puts her arms in the air and says, "Ta-da... Awesome, right?"

"I have no doubt that you can do anything you put your mind to, Ryan, but while home runs are sexy, they're not part of the plan."

"I know, but—"

Phineas interrupts. "Hall of Famer Wade Boggs had 3010 hits with a 328-lifetime batting average. He could hit home runs and did so on a regular basis at batting practice, but chose not to during games—"

Ryan says, "—Chose not to during games," together with Phineas. Ryan continues talking in a rote manner. "It throws off your eye and puts pressure on your joints. Let the home run hitters hit 235... I know. I know. The platitudes are exhausting." She removes her helmet. "I mean, don't my ideas count? When do I get to decide on things? When do I create a plan?"

Phineas looks at his watch as a tactic to conceal his shock. He then gazes at Ryan, whose look demands an answer.

"Your Uncle Rollie and I used to argue a great deal about such things."

Ryan says with regret, "I remember it well."

"But you were just a kid – a child we wanted to mold, and we needed a solid, unflappable plan to keep us on a defined path. And while that was appropriate then, you're definitely not a child anymore, and you cannot be an adult unless you're able make a decision and own the result. I'd be a failure as a parent if I didn't allow you the freedom to make your own choices. I'll say, for the record, that I still believe in the plan, but it's time for you to decide what's best for you. And it's time for me to leave. Much to my regret, as I'd much rather stay here with you. Good-bye, Ryan."

A smile forms on her face. "Good-bye, Daddy."

Phineas kisses Ryan, picks up his suitcase, then jogs to his Ferrari as Ryan puts on her helmet and walks toward home plate.

Quin, dressed in baseball attire, wakes Ryan with a soft kiss. "You were in so deep, I felt bad waking you, but I didn't want you to get up to a note."

Ryan wipes her mouth and half covers it, self-conscious of her morning breath. "I was having a dream about the last time I saw my dad."

"Didn't you see him last night?"

"Yes… Of course. It was a dream."

Quin stands. "I have to get on the road, and I won't be back 'til tomorrow night. There's food in the fridge, coffee, and a key under the mat if you want to come back."

Ryan sits up, stretching. *"Grazie."*

"After you see the quality of the—"

"I'm not thanking you for that, silly. I'm thanking you for showing me there's something in life that's even better than baseball."

"Funny," says Quin with a quick smile. "I was thinking

the same thing about you... Did I mention that the key is under the mat?"

Ryan raises her eyebrows with a jerk.

Quin smiles and walks out the door.

CHAPTER 19

Ryan is dressed in her uniform and sits across from Brick and Nelson in Brick's office.

Nelson says, "Brick, I don't want to say I told you so..."

Brick laughs. "Don't be throwing that shit up, now." Then, to Ryan, "Here's the key to your locker room, and don't forget these." He points to a pile of laminated newspapers. The top one says: *PERFECT! Ryan Stone, The First Woman in the MLB, Pitches Perfect Game!*

Ryan says, "Thank you, sir," and Brick puts pen to paper on his lineup card. "Sir?"

Brick looks up and Ryan continues, "I've worked my whole life to be a complete player. I can hit just as well as I can pitch."

"You can hit, huh?"

"Yes, sir. Singles, doubles, homers, and I can play every position except catcher."

"Ryan, I need you to go out there every five days and do like you did yesterday. I can't risk that, and pitchers can't be position players."

Ryan blurts, "With all due respect, sir, there's no such

thing as can't."

Nelson intervenes. "Ryan, let me show you to your locker—"

Brick sits up straight. "Excuse me?"

Ryan talks rapidly. "I've practiced every day of my life to pitch, hit, field, and steal. If you put me in every day, I promise you the wild card. I know it's a contract year for you—"

"What? You questioning my integrity, girl?"

"No, sir, I'd never do that. What I meant was—"

"You will do what I tell you to do, and let me make myself clear, pitching is all you'll ever do for the Greyhounds. If you win, you play, if not, I send you down. See yourself out."

Ryan nods and Nelson grabs the pile of headlines and hands them to her before she exits.

Nelson looks at Brick.

Brick says, "Hey, Nellie, you sign 'em, but I gotta deal with 'em. If you start meddlin,' you could find yo'self—"

"Who's meddlin'?"

Brick grabs a pen and starts writing again.

Nelson looks at Brick. Brick looks at Nelson and Nelson turns away, laughing.

"Whatchu laughing at? Come on now, Nellie, I got stuff to do." Brick talks to himself as he writes. "Laughin'… What the hell? I got all this shit to do and you laughin'… I tell ya."

Nelson laughs his way to the door. "You gotta admit, she's got some spunk."

Brick slaps the air. "C'mon, Nellie, go on outta here now!" He talks to himself again. "I'm trying to work and he ruinin' my concentration. The shit I gotta put up with 'round here… *Ridicilous!*"

Ryan sits on the bench for the next five days watching the

Hounds get pummeled by the Red Sox and Yankees. There are numerous occasions when she knows she could help the team by stealing a base, bunting over runners, or forcing the opposing team to change pitchers since she's a switch hitter. Ryan knows she'd contribute because she was schooled in old-style fundamentals by Rollie and her coaches in Cuba and Japan. If a team were to use a defensive shift by loading all the players to one side of the field, she has the ability to stick her bat out and punch one the opposite way. A bloop could easily become a double if no one is there to field it. She could force an opposing team out of its comfort zone in an era where most hitters are so focused on home runs, they've forgotten about the power of small ball.

Ryan's lineage and lifelong training provide the essential tools for success, but she also embodies an insatiable thirst to win, which she accomplishes on her second start of the season as she fans fifteen Yankees in a two-hit shutout. She bolsters her everyday-player argument by going three-for-three, stealing two bases, and making an acrobatic catch that is featured on highlight reels, memes, and social media platforms for a week. After her stellar performance against Yankees, however, she is relegated back to the bench as the Hounds take a short road trip, which turns out to be a dismal extension of the homestand.

Brick's frustration is such that he makes the back and front page of newspapers for getting thrown out of two games in a week. Not long after the road trip, Ryan's work with Sammy Buckets' knuckleball and Pete O'Neil's slider produces dividends as the Hounds move out of last place for the first time all season. Tree Willis also establishes himself as one of the league's premier closers. Besides Willis, Oaks, and Benny, the rest of the Hounds bond with Ryan, especially

Javy. He and Ryan spend much of their downtime together, talking about pitching, hitters, signs, and the dynamics of various ballparks.

CHAPTER 20

While several Hounds pitchers are getting loose during pre-game warm-ups in Toronto, Tree Willis and Benny Gross lean against the bullpen ledge talking. Tree is startled when a ball skins his butt. He jumps up, spins around and sees Ryan pitching to Javy.

Tree points at Ryan. "Did you do that on purpose?"

After Ryan throws a pitch, she says, "I could park a ball in the crack of your ass from thirty yards out if I wanted to, so… no."

A burst of laughter rises from nearly everyone.

Tree looks around.

Javy, cackling, takes off his mask. "Dog, my mind's crazy, yo… I picture Tree'd having to pop the ball out his ass crack with a shoehorn or sutin'."

More laughter from the crew leaves Tree speechless. Even Tree's buddy Benny smiles.

Javy stops laughing for a beat. "Wait… Wait… Tree should go to the mound, bend over, cough, and see if he can pitch a strike."

The bullpen is now belly laughing, Benny included.

Javy topples over.

Tree says, "You're a bunch of fools," and walks out. He and Ryan do their usual stare-down.

Javy, from the floor, adds, "Wait… Wait… All Tree's fots be like silent ones 'n' shit, 'cause his asshole look like a donut."

CHAPTER 21

On road trips, Ryan trains at select dōjōs and showers at her hotel, but at home she enjoys her private quarters, a former coaches' office, that's equipped with storage closets and its own bathroom and shower. Ryan, dressed in street clothes, sits on a bench in her locker room, tying her shoe.

Ito sits next to her. "I made a batch of soup yesterday. Can I drop some by your apartment?"

"Oh God, I would love that, but I'll be at Quin's for a few days and then we are on a ten- day road trip. Could you please drop it off at my freezer? ...I miss your soup."

"You may stop by the center anytime you want some home cooking."

Ryan smiles. "I'll come by more often after I get used to all of this."

"Can I take another look at your calf?"

Ryan pulls up her pant leg, revealing a huge purple, yellow, and black bruise.

"How much pain are you feeling?"

"Nothing I can't handle, plus the docs spray and wrap it before games."

BORN FOR THE GAME

Ava Locke, a woman in her fifties with blonde hair fashioned in a tight bun, enters the room. She is wearing large-rimmed black glasses, has ramrod-straight posture, and is the type of person whose presence is about as welcome as the flu. Ava holds a briefcase firmly at her side and flashes an ID badge. "Ms. Stone, I'm from Major League Baseball and I'm here to collect urine and blood to test for foreign substances... It's routine."

"Oh. Okay." Ryan stands and Ava looks at Ito.

"Please vacate the premises, sir."

Ito gives her a look and then says to Ryan, "Shall I wait outside?"

"No, thank you, Ito. I'll call you later."

Ito nods to Ryan and then exits.

Ryan holds a cotton ball on the crook of her arm and Ava places an adhesive strip over it.

Ava speaks as she grabs a plastic-covered cup from her case. "Before you produce a urine sample, I'll need you to both lift your shirt and bra up under your chin and drop your pants and underwear all the way down."

"What? Why?"

"Foreign device check."

Ryan looks at Ava for a few beats, digesting her request, then acquiesces.

"Bring your bottoms to your knees, please."

Ryan's mouth twitches as she obliges.

Ava steps behind Ryan to examine her backside.

"This is awfully thorough."

"It certainly is. People will do *anything* to cheat. Now raise your arms in the air, please."

Ryan raises her arms.

"Okay, very good. Now let's walk to the commode."

Ryan pulls her shirt down, her pants up, grabs the cup, and walks to the bathroom.

Ava trails Ryan with her briefcase in hand.

When Ryan gets to the door, she turns to Ava. "I can take it from here, thank you."

"Actually, you can't. Please sit on the commode with open legs." Ava puts on a rubber glove.

"What's with the glove?"

Ava takes the cup from Ryan. "I hold the cup, so be mindful. I don't want to get wet."

As Ryan prepares herself, Ava kneels on a towel, positions the cup, and screws her eyes in concentration.

After a minute of trying to produce a sample, Ryan asks, "Do you have to look at it like that?"

"Even if it takes all day."

Ryan closes her eyes and concentrates.

"Running tap water may be helpful, but if that doesn't move things along, I carry a few beers in my car for extreme cases. That method hasn't failed yet!"

"I don't think that'll be necessary... Just give me a minute." Ryan closes her eyes and after a few beats, tinkling is heard.

Ava smiles.

Outside Ryan's locker room is a gathering of most of her teammates, who applaud when the door opens.

Ava walks past the group with a firm grip on her briefcase and her eyes fixed forward. Ryan looks confused at first, then her mouth pops open. "Was that a prank?"

Sando shakes his head. "We wish it was."

Javy says, "Welcome to the bigs, Ryan!"

The guys surround and congratulate her.

CHAPTER 22

Ito takes a container from a shopping bag and places it in Ryan's freezer. Her one-bedroom apartment is modern LA with a splash of Japan. There's a chabudai, several bonsai trees, and a twelve-inch Buddha between two similarly sized green Taras on a wooden table.

Ito closes the freezer door, walks across the apartment, and enters Ryan's bedroom. He goes to her dresser where she has Phineas' photo positioned next to the brass cottage urn. He takes the top off and grabs one of the four ash cans. He opens it, pulls a cylinder from inside, and places it in his bag. He puts the outer container back in the urn, replaces its roof, and exits the room.

CHAPTER 23

Ryan's polyphasic sleep pattern was phased in over her first months of life and phased out to a typical sleeping pattern between her eighteenth and nineteenth birthdays in preparation for her life as a professional ballplayer. That was the only major adjustment in Ryan's routine, as she continued her practice of eating small, organic meals throughout the day and her rigorous training schedule. To compete with men, Ryan must be incredibly strong, but bulking up with weights leads to strains and tears, so she uses a two-hour-per day stretching routine created by Ito.

Ryan arrives at the ballpark early to accomplish her routine then ends each session with an hour of chanting, gratitude, and meditation.

Javy passes by her locker room early one day to compare notes before an upcoming series. He finds Ryan sitting in the lotus position to the sounds of holistic music.

"Oye, Ryan, ¿puedo entrar?" (Hey, Ryan, could I come in?)

"Por supuesto." (Of course.)

"Siempre te veo haciendo esto antes de jugar. ¿Ayudará a mi juego?" (I always see you doing this before we play. Will it

help my game?)

"Ayuda al mío." (It helps mine.) Ryan pats the space to her right. *"Siéntate aquí, cierra los ojos y sincroniza tu respiración con la mía."* (Sit here, close your eyes, and sync your breath with mine.)

Javy sits and, as he breathes together with Ryan, his shoulders and facial muscles drop and his head lolls slightly back.

"Ahora abre los brazos y concéntrate en tu respiración." (Now open your arms and focus on your breath.)

Javy continues breathing, his chest rising and falling with Ryan's.

"Si su mente divaga, devuélvala a nuestra respiración." (If your mind wanders, bring it back to our breath.)

She looks at Javy and then closes her eyes. *"Unámonos de la mano."* (Let's join hands.)

Javy clasps his hand with hers and they breathe together in rhythm.

CHAPTER 24

Brick walks the tunnel from the lockers to the dugout and squints with curiosity as he hears waves of cheers echoing off the concrete walls. He sees Nelson leaning on the dugout rail enjoying whatever is happening in the outfield. When Brick reaches the entranceway he asks, "What's all this?"

"Ryan's putting on quite a show in centerfield."

Javy smashes a ball and Ryan trails it to the deepest part of the park. She leaps, bends her arm over the wall, catches it, and rockets it home without a bounce.

Brick makes his way to the dugout phone with heavy steps and plucks the receiver off the wall. "Hey, Rocky, tell Stone I wanna see her!" He slams the handset onto the hook and it bounces off and yoyos around.

Nelson says, "I haven't seen this many fans at batting practice since I took over… This is like the old days, Brick."

"If that girl hurts her arm, we won't have fans at BP… or games, for that matter."

"You wanted to see me, Mr. Jackson?" asks Ryan as she jogs into the dugout.

"Pitchers don't shag fly balls!"

"Yes, sir." Ryan nods and sits on the far end of the bench.

Nelson talks to the field. "If this was a game and Oaksie was in center, we'd be down a run."

Brick looks at Nelson. "Well, you signed him, chief."

Nelson, still talking to the field, says, "That I did." He then turns from the field and walks away. When he's at the mouth of the tunnel, he adds, "I signed Ryan, too."

Brick looks at Nelson's back for a few beats before switching his gaze to Ryan, sitting on the bench, and looking toward the outfield.

Brick looks up at the scoreboard: Inning 8 - Texas 8 - LA 3 and then at Ryan, who sits in the same spot since he ordered her off the field during batting practice.

Brick glances at Johnny Oaks in the batting circle, swinging two bats. He then looks back at Ryan. "Hey, Ryan."

She walks over. "Yes, Mr. Jackson?"

"You're pinch hitting for Oaksie. Now, look at me when you step into the box. I'm gonna be throwing up all kinds of signs, but don't pay attention to them. Just nod your head and bunt. Got it?"

"Got it." Ryan grabs her helmet and Javy helps with her protective gear.

Brick calls out to Oaks, "Johnny, c'mon back."

Oaks jogs over and sees Ryan getting ready. "You kidding me right now? You're takin' me out for *her*?"

"Take a seat, Oaks, and see me after the game."

Oaks slams his stuff into the rack and sits next to Benny.

"And Johnny Oaks is ripping mad," says Dan Devine.

Shelly adds, "This is a gutsy move. Brick is taking out power for a probable bunt, but a bunt will move Javy into scoring position."

Ryan steps in the box and the infielders move up in anticipation of a bunt. She looks at Brick, who's going through the signs. She nods, puts the bat into the bunting position, but then pulls it back and smashes the ball down the third-base line.

Javy scores from first and Ryan slides into second base.

She calls times, brushes herself off, and kisses her locket.

Shelly can barely contain herself. "What girl in the US does not want to be Ryan Stone right now?"

"What boy doesn't want to be her?" Dan adds.

Ryan's hit kick-starts the offense. The Hounds add four more runs and eventually win the game in extra innings.

Ryan is waiting outside of Brick's office, talking to Javy and Sando, when Johnny Oaks storms out, leaving the door open.

Brick shouts out, "Stone!"

Ryan looks at Javy and Sando, confused. She enters the office and stands in front of Brick's desk, but he doesn't look up until he finishes writing.

"I told you to bunt, Stone!"

"But I saw an opportunity—"

"Well, that decision cost you five grand."

"But we won the game!"

"Make it ten grand, and if you speak again, it'll be fifteen. I don't think it takes a 197 IQ or an explanation from a Harvard professor to figure out the progression." Brick starts writing again, and Ryan stands there, speechless. Without looking up, he says, "That'll be all, Stone," and Ryan storms out.

CHAPTER 25

Ryan kicks her gym bag across Quin's room. "I cannot believe he fined me ten thousand dollars! Ten grand, Quin!"

"Well, he did, and there's nothing you can do except write the check."

"That was so wrong," says Ryan.

"I cannot change what happened, but I can suggest something that may help. It's called vodka therapy, and it works really, really well."

"If I want to relax, I meditate. It works."

"Not as well as Tito's."

After a few beats Ryan says, "I heard booze ruined your career."

Quin rubs his nose even though it doesn't itch, then looks at Ryan. "You might as well have the real story, then. I grew up in the bowels of Boston, broke as fuck, and dreaming of dollar signs. I was obsessed with making money. When the Sox gave me a million-dollar signing bonus, I knew I'd turn it into an empire. Besides my salary, there'd be endorsements, real estate investments, and restaurant chains. But while I was drunk and peeing off the tip of my new speedboat, I slipped, dislocated my shoulder, and tore up my labrum. My career was over before it started, and that sent me into a wicked tailspin which ended up in a prison cell. It was there I promised myself I'd make my fortune back one day, and I will."

"So, drinking *did* ruin your career."

"Did it?" Quin says matter-of-factly. "I was just a kid who had an accident… Most kids drink, Ryan."

"I'm sorry, Quin. I'm just being cranky. Brick can be impossible."

The two look at each other in silence for a little bit before Ryan moves to pick up her bag.

Quin says, "The appropriate response, when your boyfriend pours his heart out, is to reciprocate in some way… I know nothing about you, babe."

She places her bag on the couch. "There's not much to know, really. I was adopted by Ito and spent my life between LA, Cuba, and Japan."

"I know what you've told the press… I want to know your *secrets*."

"Quin… I like you. I really do. But I don't want anything more than what we're doing. I don't want to meet your parents, your bestie, or commit to anything. This is just for fun."

Quin feels an electric eel bite his Adam's apple.

Ryan continues, "If you need more than that, then let's end it right now."

Quin does a double-take. "Wait… Whoa… What just happened? If I overstepped, I'm sorry. What can I say, I'm just a hopeless romantic. If this is just for fun, I'll give you all the fun you want. No booze necessary." Quin moves toward Ryan with force. He picks her up, throws her over his shoulder, and walks to the bed.

"Ahhh! Put me down or I'll kick your—"

Quin throws her on the bed and tickles her.

Ryan laughs, uncontrollably. "Ahhh! Ohh! Stop it! Ahhh! Quin!"

Quin's spidery fingers jump from her ribs to her neck. "Is this fun?"

"Yes! Yes! So fun. So fun!" Ryan is practically howling now.

Quin chuckles. "And who's gonna be on top tonight?"

Ryan cannot respond because she's laughing.

Quin repeats, "I didn't hear you. Who?"

Ryan laughs through the word, *"Me!"*

Quin's fingers wiggle around to her underarms. "Who is? I missed that. I thought I heard you say, 'you.'"

Ryan responds in falsetto, "Ahhh! You! You! You're on top!"

Quin stops tickling Ryan and the two look at each other for a few beats, then kiss, hungrily.

CHAPTER 26

Tree Willis and Johnny Oaks walk into an empty locker room. They hear soft music and follow the sound to the entrance of Ryan's area, where most of the team, including Benny Gross, is meditating.

Tree laughs then blurts out, "What's this, a Shaolin temple?"

Ryan rises and gets in his face. "Anytime you want to finish what you started at the open tryout, Tree."

Javy gets between them and Tree points at Ryan. "You think you're tough, little girl, because men don't want to get into trouble, but I dare you to throw a punch at me. I will smack the living shit out of you."

Brick comes out of his office. "What the hell's goin' on out here?"

Tree walks away with Oaks.

Brick shouts, "Everybody outside for BP."

The players head to their lockers, throwing daggers at Tree.

Brick touches Javy's shoulder and cocks his head in the direction of his office.

The tension between Ryan and Tree foreshadows the

game that follows. The Hounds and Minnesota are in a zero-zero stalemate until Buckets throws a ball that catches too much of the plate and it gets deposited in the bleacher seats. In the bottom of the ninth, Javy has a twelve pitch at bat and gets on first with a lead-off walk, then Oaks strikes out.

Brick looks at Ryan on the bench. "Hey, Ryan."

Ray White swings and pops it up as Ryan approaches Brick.

"Yes, sir?"

"Take this guy long."

"Yes, sir."

Shelly Shaw looks at Dan. "Brick is putting in Ryan? They need a home run right now and Ryan hasn't homered all year. I don't get it."

"I can't say I disagree, Shelly."

Ryan digs in at home plate and Minnesota's big closer throws smoke. Ryan takes a healthy cut, but misses.

"She's swinging for the seats, Shelly. No doubt about that."

After Ryan tips off the next ball, Shelly says, "She is clearly overpowered."

Ryan bears down and rocks to and fro, focusing on the pitcher as he gets the sign, nods, and winds up. The pitcher releases the ball and Ryan sees it as clearly as if it were in slow motion. The ball drops, Ryan gets on top of it, and hits a grounder to the second baseman, who fields it and throws her out.

"That was a nasty slider, folks," explains Dan, "but that's it. Ryan's magic runs out as the Hounds lose 1-0 and waste a Sammy Buckets gem."

Ryan watches Minnesota celebrate from first base. She then walks slowly to the dugout where Brick is waiting for her. "I'm sorry, Mr. Jackson."

"Why you sorry? I asked you to swing away. You did your job."

"I told you I could hit homers."

"I'm sure you can. But even Hank Aaron couldn't hit one out every time."

"Thank you, Mr. Jackson."

"You great, Ryan... Maybe the best I ever seen, at this point in your career. But you still a damn rookie." His chuckle makes Ryan smile. He adds, "There'll be a time when you make your own choices, but 'til then, you just listen to me."

As Ryan turns to leave, Brick says, "It's all good, kid," and sends her off with a sporty butt slap.

Just after his hand makes contact, he pulls it back and flashes a look of horror. "Oh, damn, Ryan. I didn't mean to—"

"It's cool, Mr. Jackson. I know it was just a reaction, and that's what's so cool about it. For a moment, there, you didn't see me as a girl. You saw me as a ballplayer... and... thanks for believing in me tonight." Ryan winks and walks into the tunnel.

CHAPTER 27

Los Angeles Times:

TREE WILLIS AND JOHNNY OAKS TRADED TO RIVAL SAN FRANCISCO WAVES. RYAN STONE SET TO PLAY CENTERFIELD.

B rick meets with Nelson to discuss the tension between Ryan, Tree, and Oaks, and it's decided that the tension must go. The Tree/Oaks trade brought with it the benefits of both getting Ryan on the field every day and giving the team an opportunity to gel. While the Hounds organization is confident about the roster move, there are naysayers who provide sports talk-shows with an abundance of content, but Ryan's heroics quickly flip the dialog.

While Ryan begins drawing comparisons to the greatest centerfielders of all time, none of them could compete with her acrobatic ability or the accuracy of her throwing arm. Opposing teams' respect for her is so great, she all but snuffs out their ability to score when the ball is hit in her direction, and Ryan's gymnastics training turns a baseball game into a show, with fans getting crazed whenever Ryan catches a ball while in mid-air or when she flips head-over-heels to snag one that's nearly out of reach. While Ryan became a national sensation as a pitcher, having her play every day makes her a national obsession, and the whole country is excited about baseball again.

Opposing teams are warned by ownership not to throw at her, as Ryan is good for business. Revenue spikes on everything from team apparel to attendance, and there is also an influx of Little Leaguers and school teams, which blow up in numbers due to an increase of female athletes.

Ryan also provides a unifying camaraderie in a nation divided by political views and a struggling economy. Local and national media of all genres dedicate slots in their shows for Ryan as they watch the Hounds go from a team with the worst record in baseball to a legitimate contender. With all the media attention, Ryan hires an agency, with Ito acting as her manager, so she can concentrate on baseball. Ryan is on talk shows, in TV commercials, and featured on magazine covers, all while leading her group of mismatched underdogs to their first playoff berth in over twenty years.

The front page of the *LA Times* has a cartoon showing the team piled high on Ryan's back as she breaks though a finish-line-ribbon with the words "Wild Card" written across it. The headline above the cartoon reads:

STONE'S 12TH INNING SINGLE SENDS DOGS TO THE PLAYOFFS!

A Hounds fanbase grows and "Stone 34" T-shirts as well as all Hounds' apparel are selling out all over the world. Ryan is happy that everything is going so well, but she is frustrated because Phineas isn't there to see it. She could get accolades from fans, media, or even heads of state, but its value is diminished, as she wants to hear it from the one who matters most.

CHAPTER 28

The night the Hounds clinch a wild-card spot, the locker room has a positive vibe, but there are no Champagne baths or tomfoolery. Ryan proposes that the Hounds only celebrate a World Series victory. The team agrees and do post-game interviews for the sake of the fans and the network, but outsiders are escorted away at a specified time. Nelson and Brick are informed that the meeting is for players only, and they, too, must exit the locker room. Once the team has cleaned up, they talk freely about the season and what it would mean to them if they won it all. Some state frankly that they are playing for the financial freedom of a fat contract, but most of them talk about winning more for others than for themselves. They mention children, wives, parents, siblings, aunts, uncles, grandparents, friends, and God.

Sando brings his teammates to tears when he speaks of his twin brother, Vincent. He says the two played stickball and baseball together in the Bay Ridge section of Brooklyn where they were raised, and that Vincent was the better ballplayer. Sando says this isn't a sentimental opinion. Vincent received a full baseball scholarship to UCLA, while

BORN FOR THE GAME

Sando had to pay to play. When Vincent was diagnosed with pancreatic cancer in his sophomore year, he was one hundred ninety pounds of muscle, but wound up a gray, ninety-two-pound skeleton at the time of his death just six months later. Baseball was the highlight of Vincent's life and Sando promised his brother that he'd win a World Series ring for him one day.

Ryan is the last to speak and she uses broad strokes to describe both how much it means to be on this team and that she will win this series to honor her father. She closes the session by leading the team in a gratitude chant where they have an opportunity to shout out who or what they are thankful for. They hug each other and go straight home because they scheduled a voluntary team practice the following morning.

CHAPTER 29

Ryan and Ito glance at room numbers as they walk through the UCLA Medical Center.

Ryan is holding a bunch of flowers. "I'm still shocked he asked to see me."

"I cannot imagine anyone *not* wanting to." Ito points to a door and they turn into a large, single room. Sitting up in bed is Dakota Swiftwater. He has a beaming smile and a nasal cannula device supplying oxygen to his nostrils.

Ryan says, "Hello, Mr. Swiftwater. It's such an honor to meet you."

Dakota, smiling, stares at Ryan long enough to make her slightly uncomfortable. He then says, "I didn't think it possible, but you are even more beautiful in person than you are on TV."

Ryan gives him a quick head bow. "Thank you, sir. Thank you very much... Oh... May I put these flowers next to you, there?"

Dakota nods.

Ryan approaches and places the flowers on a table near a large scrapbook.

Dakota pats a space on the bed next to him.

Ryan looks at Ito before taking a seat.

Dakota inhales deeply, then takes his eyes off Ryan for the first time and looks at Ito. "How are you, Ito?"

"I'm doing well, Dakota."

"You didn't tell me you knew Dakota Swiftwater."

Dakota looks at Ryan. "I've been following your career very closely. I imagine you'll break all of my records, except maybe my home-run record." He laughs a little, then begins coughing. Ryan fills a water glass from a pitcher and hands it to him.

Dakota takes a few sips and regains his composure. "Thank you, Ryan... Can you hand me that, please?" He points to the large scrapbook.

Ryan hands him the book and he motions for her to move closer on the bed.

The book is an assemblage of newspaper and magazine articles about Ryan, who's a little spooked by it. As she turns the pages, she realizes that the book follows her career from her first day until the present.

Dakota says in a whispery voice, "There's more." He then turns through several blank pages to a page filled with old, cracked black-and-white photos of strangers.

Ryan points to a photo of a woman dressed in a glittery leotard. She's posing with her arms held daintily in the air. "She is very beautiful. Is this your mother?"

"She's Alla Yudovich, a woman from a family of Russian Jewish trapeze artists, and, yes, she's my mother, Ryan... and your grandmother."

Ryan looks to Ito with a wrinkled brow but quickly turns back to Dakota, whose eyes are dripping with tears.

Ryan asks, "Are you...?"

"Yes, Ryan. I'm your father."

Ryan looks back at Ito. "This is true?" Ito nods and Ryan hugs Dakota tenderly as she repeats, "Oh my God!" several times as she sobs. After a long moment, she pulls back and studies his face. She gently touches his cheek with her fingers, then Dakota wipes his tears with his pajama sleeve and moves over in the bed. Ryan slides in close to him and wipes her eyes, as well.

Dakota grabs the book, opens it, and points to a picture on the page. "This man here is your grandfather, Satanta."

Ito quietly exits the room and Dakota continues, "Satanta was a proud Kiowa Indian."

CHAPTER 30

A paunchy man in his late fifties with an outrageous handlebar mustache, blue-and-red polka-dot suspenders, and a tangled mess of curly black hair walks through a bustling newsroom holding a cup of coffee and a briefcase. He moves toward a desk with a ringing phone, puts down his coffee, and picks up the receiver. "Jenson here... Hello?" He hangs up, opens his briefcase, and takes out a laptop and a newspaper with the headline that reads, *Dakota Swiftwater Dead at 97.*

His phone rings again. "Jenson here." He smiles. "How are you, sir?" His expression changes. "What?" He looks around and lowers his voice. "Do you have proof?"

CHAPTER 31

While Ryan is driving, she dabs her eyes, blows her nose, and tosses the tissue on her car's seat along with the Dakota newspaper story. Her cell rings and Quin's picture appears on the display. She picks up, sniffles, and says, "Hey."

"It sounds like you heard the news."

"What news?"

"Don't go to my house, it's swarming with paparazzi. I'm at the Belmore Hotel, room 402. Meet me there."

Ito is transfixed to his TV screen.

The reporter says, "Ryan Stone, the first female in the MLB, the MVP of the ALCS, and tomorrow's World Series Game 1 pitcher, is the genetic experiment of flamboyant billionaire and accused murderer Phineas Stone, who paid off the late Dakota Swiftwater and Olympic Champion Valentina Fermi in an attempt to manufacture a super athlete."

Nelson stands in his office watching the news on his wall of flatscreens.

"Dakota Swiftwater was seventy-seven and Valentina Fermi only twenty-six when they coupled to create Stone. With us tonight is Bishop Joseph McCoy of Oakland."

A silver-haired man with a buzzcut and a scowl speaks into a microphone. "The Church does not condone experiments attempting to create a superior human being. The Holocaust was the result of such an ideology."

Ryan and Quin watch the report from their hotel room.

A field reporter holds a microphone in front of a group of boisterous young men outside of the San Francisco Waves Stadium.

A haughty youth speaks into the microphone, "I read that Ryan's freakish strength is linked to testosterone and HGH injections. We all knew she had to be on something, but no one wanted to admit it, publicly."

The reporter faces the camera with a practiced dramatic pose. "Such reports are unconfirmed at this time, but Major League Baseball is reinvestigating Stone's blood and urine samples and Tweeted that Stone will face serious consequences if the testing reveals foreign substances."

The scene switches back to recorded footage of Brick waving away reporters as he gets into a car.

The anchor says, "Neither manager Brick Jackson nor anyone from the Greyhounds organization has yet to make a statement."

Ryan shuts off the TV and paces. "Drugs? Are they kidding me? I cannot believe this is happening. Can they plant anything in my samples? Can they do that sort of thing?"

Quin says, "I don't think—"

"My head's going to explode, Quin. I can't stop the circular thoughts!"

Quin puts on his jacket. "I'm going out for some food and a bottle of booze. Lie down and chill till I get back, and whatever you do, don't turn on the TV." Quin kisses her and exits.

As soon as the door closes, Ryan clicks on the TV.

Several half-eaten Chinese food containers are on a table and a quart of fried rice has spilled over onto Ryan's shirt, which is lying on the floor next to an empty bottle of Absolut 100 vodka.

Quin is sleeping under the covers and Ryan lies naked on her stomach on the opposite side of the bed, her arm dangling off the edge. She opens her eyes and coughs before vomiting into a half-filled bucket. She then slides onto the floor for a few minutes, holding her stomach.

Ryan sits up, rubbing her eyes. "My God, Quin. How will I pitch tonight? My stomach is on fire... And my head!" She holds her head with both hands for a few minutes before she uses the bed for support to stand. Hunched over, she gathers her clothes on the way to the bathroom. Pieces of rice are stuck to her shirt.

"You need to drink some milk."

Ryan calls out from the bathroom, "Why did you let me do that to myself?"

Quin gets up and speaks to the door. "Wait a minute... Don't you put this on me, Ryan, you're a big girl."

"You've been pushing me to drink since I met you." Coughing is followed by dry heaves.

"Again, Ryan. It was your decision. Your choice. You were having a great time."

Ryan comes out of the bathroom dressed and gets in his face. "You should've dumped the bottle once you saw me getting too drunk." She holds her head.

"That's right, just keep blaming me, Ryan... Look... Ryan... my landlord called and he's giving me a lot of shit because the neighbors are complaining about the paparazzi, who will not leave the property. I didn't sign up for this."

"And what's that supposed to mean, Quin?"

"It means I don't want my life turned into a circus. This was just for fun, right? Well, it's not fun anymore."

"You son of a bitch! You rotten son of a bitch!" Ryan grabs her keys and bag off a table and slams the door as she exits.

CHAPTER 32

W hile driving, Ryan sniffles as she rubs her temple and slides her hand down her face and past her chin. She slams on the brakes while frantically feeling around her neck. A truck screeches and nearly rear-ends her.

Ito is talking on his cell while driving. "Calm down, Ryan. I cannot understand you."

Ryan paces outside her car in an empty lot. "I lost my locket, got drunk with Quin last night, and I'm puking up a little blood... No, just little specks of red... I did, and Quin checked the room, already," she replies in answer to his question.

Ito says, "Drink lukewarm miso soup with turmeric and sit in a bath. Tell Quin... He broke up with you? Okay, stay calm. I'll find the locket and take care of everything else. I have to go. Remember, warm soup with turmeric, warm baths, and rest. I'll call you as soon as I can. Bye." Ito turns off the LAX exit.

Nelson stands at a podium in the Greyhounds' pressroom, facing a packed audience of reporters who wave microphones at him. Nelson points to a reporter.

"Mr. Hernandez, is Ryan Stone taking illegal substances?"

Nelson pauses before speaking. "Miss Stone has been tested far more frequently than any player on my team. It was getting to the point where we were talking to the commissioner about potential sex discrimination, and since you wrote an article about it, I don't know why you'd ask me such a question." Nelson addresses the group. "And for the record, every one of you in this room," he wags an accusing finger, "should be ashamed of yourselves, digging into that girl's family and vomiting your scurrilous trash all over the media. Why Ryan's parents got together has nothing to do with her, and it's really none of anyone's business." Nelson leaves the podium to a hailstorm of questions.

Brick looks at Ryan's blood-shot eyes from across his desk. "Did you sleep at all last night?"

Ryan nods and takes a sip from a paper hot cup.

Brick continues, "God knows you've been through a lot, and there ain't nobody that counts who's gonna blame you if you can't pitch tonight."

"There's no 'can't,' Mr. Jackson."

"Right. You've mentioned that on various occasions. Look me in the eyes, Ryan, and if you tell me you're okay, I'm going to trust your word."

CHAPTER 33

The outside of Quin's apartment complex has approximately thirty-five feet of scratchy lawn leading to a horizontal row of tired, spindly palm plants attempting to act as a privacy border between the complex and the sidewalk.

While walking along a frayed slate path, Quin hears clicking against the sidewalk on the other side of the palm-plant border. He looks, but can only make out a group of figures in the dwindling light, walking together in a tight ball. A vehicle pulls up, the car doors open, slam closed, and a black Mercedes SUV speeds away.

Quin sticks his key into his front door, then rushes into a violated, tossed apartment. Clothes are scattered about, and what few drawers he has have been emptied, including his cash stash, which litters the floor along with pens, papers, screws, and other misfit items. Quin moves to his desk where his laptop had been. He picks up the mouse. "Shit!"

Quin hears something behind him and he spins around to find Ito moving toward him.

At Greyhound Stadium, Ryan is on the pitcher's mound scanning the loud, packed ballpark. She notices a sign saying

"Ryanstein." Another one says, "Man-made Stone," and a group is posed in the Hitler salute.

She reaches for her missing locket and the umpire yells, "Play ball!"

Ryan takes her cap off, wipes her sweaty brow with her forearm, slips her hat back on, and peers at Javy for the sign.

Willy Stubbs wiggles his bat in a circular motion while looking at Ryan with malice.

The crowd's screams squeeze Ryan's throbbing head as she winds up fast and pitches a slow knuckleball.

Willy crushes it.

Quin lands on his small table and it explodes into pieces. He grabs one of the table legs like a club.

Johnny Oaks smashes a ball.

El Caballo jacks one out of the stadium and it bounces off the Greyhounds office building.

Quin swings the table leg at Ito, but he blocks it and returns the favor by knocking Quin out with a spin kick.

Ito pats him down, finds his cell, holds it to Quin's face, and it opens. He then takes a piece of paper from his pocket and taps numbers and symbols into the cell.

Rollie is sitting in his living room, watching the game. There's a closeup of a disheveled Ryan on the mound.

Rollie's cell rings and the word "Quin" appears on the screen. He swipes it on. "Yes, Quin."

"It's not Quin. It's Ito."

Rollie digests this for a moment. "Can you put Quin on?"

"He's indisposed at the moment."

"I see. Ya know, it's so funny, Ito, but I was gonna call you tonight."

Ito is on the floor next to Quin, who's beginning to rouse.

"I have to go, but, yes, I'll meet you in an hour." Ito hangs up, puts Quin's cell on the floor, and places him in a choke-hold until he goes limp. Ito grabs duct tape and a cellphone from his backpack. He puts the tape aside then dials a number and says, "I'm meeting him in an hour."

Ryan looks at Brick though weary eyes as he approaches the mound.

Javy pats her on the shoulder just before Brick puts his hand out.

Ryan places the ball in Brick's open palm and she jogs off to a thunderstorm of cheers and boos.

Rollie lounges comfortably in a booth in a dark corner of an old-man bar. He sucks down a bronze-colored drink from a rock glass as Ito approaches. Rollie gestures to the bench across from him and Ito slides in.

"Oh, Ito, before we begin, power off your cell." Ito complies and Rollie holds his hand out for the phone. He checks Ito's device, gives it back, and says, cheerfully, "Do you know Elvis Presley's manager, the Colonel, got fifty percent of all of Elvis' earnings?"

"And why would I care?"

Rollie smiles. "Because I'm Ryan's new manager, you're out of a job, and from now on, I get fifty percent of everything she makes. And I mean *everything* – salary, endorsements, appearances on... I don't know, Sesame Street and what have you. Well, technically, I get forty percent and Quin gets ten, but those are minor details."

"I guess the alcohol destroyed what few brain cells you had left."

Rollie motions to a pruny cocktail waitress, points to his drink, then looks at Ito. "I can handle mine, but Ryan...? Not so much. You see, Quin made a very close-up, very explicit, well-lit video of last night's sexcapades… and Ryan puts on quite the show indeed."

Ito grits his teeth as Rollie continues. "I either release the video to my newspaper guy for a fair sum, or Ryan signs my contract." He grabs a stack of papers from his seat and puts it on the table. "And she doesn't have much time, because if this is not signed by midnight tonight, there will be a much bigger story about Ryan Stone tomorrow… besides the one about her getting a shellacking in tonight's game."

"This is what you've always wanted, isn't it?"

"I knew I'd win eventually, and it's really best for Ryan that I did. I'll make her far more money than what she would have ever earned with you or her meathead father."

"Ryan's mother told us to call if we ever needed her, and to refresh your diseased mind, she creates the most advanced technology in the world. When you answered Quin's call, all your files were locked."

Rollie scrolls through his phone then puts it in his pocket and chuckles. "So she did. Well, whoopty-fucking-doo. Ms. Fermi might have an IQ of a zillion, but I'm craftier than her, you, or Phineas."

"Do you really think so?"

Rollie looks at Ito for a few beats before his face drops. He grabs the contract and bolts toward the door, nearly toppling the elderly waitress.

Ito dials his cell. "He just left."

Rollie's car screeches to a halt in front of his complex. He jumps out, runs toward his apartment, and trips over his own feet. He gets up and limps the rest of the way to his door, which is slightly ajar. He pushes it open and shouts, "Oh no! God, no!" His apartment appears as if it imploded. He runs to the bedroom and frantically reaches under his mattress. He pulls out a note reading *"Grazie."* He punches the bed repeatedly with both fists, squawks eerily, then gets up and begins throwing and breaking anything he touches.

CHAPTER 34

Ryan's bathroom door has steam rolling out of it from a running shower. The cell phone on her dresser plays lively theme music as an overzealous radio host jumps in…

"All… righty!" He vocalizes the last notes of the music, off key, "Da-da-da-da-da… daaaa! I'm Jimmy Dee and we are back to talk about the only thing anyone is talking about, and that's tonight's final game of the most exciting World Series in memory. It's been a gloves-off, in-your-face street fight, and what's most amazing is that the Hounds have been grinding out wins despite Ryan Stone's collapse. While manager Brick Jackson has been loyal to Stone thus far, he's not announced a starting pitcher for tonight's deciding game seven. Our Fan Forum Question of the Day is, Should Ryan Stone Pitch Tonight? Our first caller is Debbie Swanson from Santa Monica. Debbie, the stage is yours."

Debbie's voice sounds as though she is in a tunnel. "Ryan should definitely pitch tonight because she carried the Hounds to the Freeway Series. They were in last place before she joined them, and they would still be there if it weren't for her. It'd be wrong of Brick Jackson to deny her the start."

"Thanks so much, Debbie! I know there are many who feel the way you do, but I'm a little less sentimental. We have a shot to win now, so loyalty, as far as I'm concerned, is off the table…

Caller two is Gavin from Palo Alto. Whatcha got for us, my man?"

"I agree with the girl. I think Ryan should pitch tonight so the Waves can beat her up again." Jimmy Dee laughs. "It's been a lot of fun watching that."

"I hear you, man, but as everyone knows, my veins bleed Greyhound red and gray."

A squeaking sound is heard in the bathroom before the shower stops.

"And next on the line is José from Hollywood. What's your take, brother?"

José clears his throat. "Hey, man, thanks for having me on. I listen to you every day, but yeah, I'm a Mets fan, so I'm looking at it without prejudice. It's been fun to watch this series, but it makes no difference to me who wins it. That said, Brick Jackson would be CRAZY, and I mean CRAZY, to put Ryan on the mound tonight. I don't care how good she was, she's in a funk right now. Maybe the league's caught up with her."

Ryan walks out of the bathroom wearing leggings and a V-neck tee. As José continues his rant, she switches the station to yoga music before completing her daily ritual of braiding her hair and doing a quick stretching routine. She shuts off the music, stops at her dresser mirror, and studies herself. She moves closer and closer, looking directly into her eyes until she is inches from the glass. Her somber, elegiac expression remains unaffected until she backs away and switches her gaze to the photo of Phineas, looking at it just as deeply as she had looked at herself. She touches the smoking urn, speaks to it with silently moving lips, then turns with a soldier's precision, grabs her backpack and hoodie off the bed, and exits the room.

Ryan approaches Phineas' old shoe-shine location with her head buried deep in a frayed hoodie that Ito bought from a homeless man. He laundered it and gave it to Ryan so she could move about incognito. She stops and sees the shadowy figure of her father buffing Mr. Walcott's shoes. The ghostly Mr. Walcott gives Phineas a coin and Phineas tips his cap.

Mr. Walcott says, *"Will you be here tomorrow, son?"*

"As long as it doesn't rain."

Mr. Walcott smiles and clumps to an awaiting limo.

Ryan looks past the limo to the grandiose lettering of *Walcott Hotels*, which has been replaced by the smaller, more discreet, *Schiff Technologies.* Ryan heads toward Ito's center.

Ryan and Ito kneel on cushions at the chabudai. Ryan finishes her bowl of soup with a slurp.

Ito smiles. "I'm glad you liked it!"

"Remember when I was a kid and you told me that the Buddha taught you how to make soup and I believed you?"

Ito laughs. "Yes, but you were not gullible for very long." He reaches into his pocket. "I have something for you." He opens his hand and reveals her diamond locket.

Ryan's mouth gapes. "Where did you find it?" She takes the locket from Ito with cupped hands then spreads it out by holding it at each end.

"I didn't. Your mother found it at Rollie's apartment, under his mattress."

"Oh my God! I just got a chill."

Ito takes the necklace from Ryan, drapes in on her neck,

and clasps it.

Ryan holds the heart against her chest. "My little-girl fantasy of my mother saving me from the scary monsters of life actually happened."

"Yes, it did."

"This is going to sound strange, Ito, but even though I've never met her, I have a connection... a palpable... I don't know... It's like when I met Dakota... I felt a warmth that I can only describe as love. I know Daddy had a deal, but if he were here, I'd beg him to let me meet her."

Ito smiles. "Who would've thought that Rollie would be the one to bring your mother into your life, and in such a way? He is also the one who suggested Dakota as a possible father for you. Despite all the crimes he's committed, you simply wouldn't be alive if it weren't for Rollie."

"Don't even mention his name, Ito. I cannot understand how he could do such disgusting things... How can a person change like that?"

"It's no mystery, Ryan. Rollie couldn't forgive... and that is cancer of the soul. It festered inside of him for years, eating away the layers of who he once was... This is what's left."

Ryan raises her voice. "I honestly don't care. I really... just cannot believe this happened to me."

"Is that your choice?"

"Choice? It's not a choice, it's reality!"

Ito returns to his place opposite Ryan at the chabudai. "Perception is a choice. What we choose to think shapes our perceptions and, ultimately, our reality." Ryan looks confused and Ito continues, "The distance between the mound and the mitt is still sixty feet six inches. The ball weighs five ounces, and has two hundred sixteen stitches. Those things haven't changed. Your *choices* have. They've created the baggage affecting your release point, your timing, your serenity."

Ito finishes his soup with a slurp and Ryan looks down for a while, making tiny circles on the floor with her index finger. She makes eye contact with Ito for a beat, then shoots to her feet and walks to the door. She slips on her shoes and says, with a quick head bow, *"Gochisousama deshita."* (An expression meaning "Thank you for the food." Food can be a metaphor for one's advice or one's graciousness.)

Ito bows his head and Ryan exits.

Rollie, unshaved and unkempt, sleeps on a chair in his apartment in front of a television. There are newspapers, empty beer cans, pizza boxes, paper dishes, cups, shards of reflective glass, and plastic utensils mixed in with the debris scattered by Valentina's crew. He's roused awake by pounding. He looks at his watch and then staggers to the door and opens it.

Ryan stands there tall and strong, her locket visible and sparkling proudly in the crook of her V-neck shirt.

He avoids her glance. "Is Ito here?"

She doesn't answer.

"The police? Nelson Rodriguez?"

"Look at me, Uncle Rollie."

Rollie continues his blank, downward gaze.

"Look at me!"

Rollie raises his eyes to hers, and asks, with trepidation, "Why do you call me uncle?"

Ryan continues her frigid stare until a burst of body odor betrays Rollie's attempt at composure. His bottom lip pushes up, then quivers just before it all gives way.

"I'm so sorry, Ryan! I'm so sorry... I... lost my mind, baby. I can't even look at myself. I broke all the mirrors in the apartment." He looks away, holding his head. "I could never expect you to forgive me. I…" He babbles gibberish before he turns to walk back into his loathsome, dilapidated room.

"I have forgiven you, Uncle Rollie."

Rollie turns and moves to hug Ryan, but she blocks him.

"I forgive you, but I can never forget what you did to me. I can also never forget what you did *for* me. You made me into the player I am. You taught me things my father and Ito could never have taught me, and I will never forget that."

Rollie's eyebrows crunch into a wrinkly V and he hugs Ryan tightly, his chin clamps onto her shoulder, but Ryan neither hugs him nor pushes him away. After a few moments, he unhooks himself and looks at her with the vulnerable eyes of a child.

Ryan says, "Goodbye, Uncle Rollie," and walks away.

Rollie bows his head and slumps back into his chair without bothering to close the door.

Loud guttural sobs burst from the room as Ryan walks the path to her car and drives away.

CHAPTER 35

Ryan pulls into the Greyhound players' lot and gets out of her car to a dense throng of reporters who pelt her with questions as she walks, head down, toward the building. Four enormous security guards rush out, encircle Ryan, and blow through the reporter pack.

Once in the building, Ryan walks to her locker with razor focus and robust strides.

A stadium worker pulls a hand truck of paper goods up several ramps into a food booth called the Hound House, where he stocks the items. Next to him is another worker, stuffing packages of hot dog buns under the counter.

Four umpires, one wearing a backwards baseball cap, play cards in a private room equipped with a large flatscreen, showers, an accessories closet, and several lockers. There is a tray of sandwiches next to a coffee machine, water cooler, and refrigerator.

A boy and a girl dressed in Greyhounds uniforms load bats into slots in the dugout. Another boy sweeps the floor with a push broom and a girl places boxes of bubble gum and peanuts along the bench.

Ryan bends around a turn to her locker room and is

greeted by her teammates.

Javy says, "We're ready to medi, bruh."

Ryan's teammates high-five her, tap her on the shoulder, or wave as they pile into her room.

Sando comes by with a case of Fuji water. "Hey, Rye, I thought you'd like this particular variety."

Ryan winks and walks into the room as her teammates form a circle on the floor.

Javy clicks his cell a few times until yoga music plays. He places the phone inside a cup then joins his teammates.

Waves manager Gil Todd is surrounded by reporters in the visitors' locker room.

A female reporter asks, "Your record against Ryan Stone is two and one, but the loss was a perfect game. Are you concerned about the possibility of facing her with the World Series on the line?"

Gil chuckles. "Absolutely not. That first game was a fluke because we were not prepared for her style of pitching. Once we had an opportunity to study the analytics, we proved that she's no threat. We knocked her out of two games in the past week… But why are we talking about Ryan Stone? She's a non-issue. My guys are feeling good about whoever they face tonight."

From a distance, the stadium resembles a giant ant farm as thousands of fans move in flowing lines through ramps, aisles, and seating rows while platoons of camera people position themselves strategically around the park.

Dan Devine and Shelly Shaw perform their pre-game show.

"That's right, Shelly. With the exception of San Francisco's game-one blowout, every contest featured extra-inning play, which was capped by last night's fifteen-inning marathon, decided on an El Caballo moon shot at 1:06 this morning."

"On paper, the Waves are the superior team," says Shelly with a finger in the air, "but games are not decided on paper. And another point to consider is that if the Hounds hadn't traded Tree Willis and Johnny Oaks to the Waves, this'd be a very different series, indeed."

"Well, Shelly, it'll all be settled tonight, but the Hounds have yet to announce a starting pitcher. The big question is, will it be Ryan Stone?"

"You'll be on the bench tonight, Stone," says Brick, looking firmly at Ryan from across his desk.

"The bench?"

"A 20.4 series ERA coupled with an .53 batting average means you haven't healed, and it would be irresponsible of me to put you out there."

"But I—"

Brick cuts her off. "I can't afford to play you… and tonight… there *is* a 'can't.'"

"I understand why you'd think this is best, but I swear on my father that I'm okay. You can trust me, Mr. Jackson."

"I been trusting you," says Brick sympathetically, "but that's the competitor in you talking, and I respect the shit outta you for it, but managers need to have eyes when their players can't see."

"But sir—"

"Your season's over."

Ryan takes a few steps toward the door, turns back, and speaks as she approaches. "Mr. Jackson, if your vision is twenty-twenty, then why can't you see the fire in my eyes?" Ryan has her hands on Brick's desk. "I'm asking you to please, sir, look again."

Ryan sits on the bench wearing her warmup jacket as Sammy Buckets leads the Hounds onto the field.

Ito stands at his loge seat a few levels up behind home plate, scanning the field for Ryan with a hand above his eyes like a salute. When he spots her on the bench, he eases himself into his seat.

Nelson looks for Ryan from his office through a pair of binoculars. When he sees her benched, he pounds the glass with his fist.

Gil Todd looks at Ryan from the visitors' dugout. and says, "That's right missy, sit your little ass on that bench and leave it to the boys."

Shelly Shaw talks into the mic. "This is a challenge for Sammy Buckets. He's had a great series, but he pitched two days ago and did an inning last night – well, technically this morning – but champions will always find another gear when there's only fumes left in the tank."

"True, Shelly, and even though Ryan Stone is the reason why the Hounds are here, she is also the reason why the staff is hurting, as she's been knocked out of both starts before the third inning."

The umpire shouts the game into action, pulls down his mask, and Sammy Buckets peers in for the sign with shiny half-moons of sweat under his eyes. He exchanges the ball from his glove to his hand, positions his right foot against the rubber, kicks his left knee up to his chest, and fires a slider.

Willy Stubbs whacks it up the middle for a hard single.

Gil Todd claps and shouts to Johnny Oaks, "They dumped you, Johnny Boy, and now it's payback time."

Sammy Buckets wipes the sweat off his face with his forearm, rests the gloved ball on his knee, checks Javy for the sign, holds the set, and then tosses a fastball, which Oaks strokes down the first-base line for a double.

"That was not a bad pitch, Dan. Oaks went with it and flicked it down the line. That's a nice piece of hitting. And the Hounds are in a jam two batters in."

"Without a doubt, Shelly. There are men on second and third with no outs and the red-hot El Caballo is coming up. Do you know his series average with men in scoring position?"

"Not exactly, but it's got to be over 450."

"You're close. 467. And so, *mi amiga*, we are in the top half of the first and we already have a crucial at bat."

El Caballo steps in and rips a 3-1 pitch off the top of the wall for a triple.

Willy and Oaks high-five at the plate, and Gil smacks their butts as they enter the dugout.

The Beard walks up to the plate, and Gil shouts, "Keep the carousel moving!"

Johnny Oaks cups his hands and shouts, "Hey, Ryan, how's that bench feeling?"

Willy Stubbs gives Oaks a double-handed high-five.

Ryan takes a slug of water and looks straight ahead.

Dan says, with a quick shake of his head, "And just like that, it's two nothing."

The Beard hits a sacrifice fly to deep center and El Caballo crosses the plate.

"Make that three nothing, Dan."

Brick looks up at the scoreboard. It reads 3-0 in the first. He looks up at it again and it's 4-0 in the third. He calls time out and walks to the mound, tapping his right arm.

Sammy Buckets walks off and Pete O'Neill takes the ball from Brick. His first pitch gets clobbered and Brick drops his head. He takes off his cap, scratches his head, replaces his cap, and looks at the field again.

Nelson Hernandez throws his hands up when Sando bobbles a ball at shortstop.

O'Neill kicks the mound dirt.

Javy calls time and waves the infield to the mound. "Yo, let's not lose our heads. We've come too far to blow up like this."

Sando says, "I should have had that, guys."

"No problem. We're all under pressure here," O'Neill assures him.

The umpire approaches the mound. "Let's play ball."

The Hounds clap and trot back to their positions.

The scoreboard ticks from 4-0 to 5-0.

"Tack on another run for the Waves," says Dan. "This game's turning ugly."

"Yes, it is," agrees Shelly. "They look exhausted out there, lifeless."

Ryan gets off the bench and walks across the dugout. She passes Brick and says, without looking at him, "I'll be warming up."

Brick watches Ryan walk into the tunnel. He then calls time, walks onto the field tapping his left arm, and Benny Gross jogs out of the bullpen.

Ryan grunts as she tosses powerful pitches into the shock-absorbing blanket in the underground cages.

Benny Gross gets the sign from Javy. He checks the runner on second, winds up, and tosses one high and outside.

The umpire shouts, "Ball!"

Sweat drips down Benny's face as Javy throws down the sign.

Ryan wipes away sweat with the back of her hand before

she punishes the blanket with another bullet.

Dan speaks softly into his mic. "And there are men on first and second with no outs in the top of the seventh."

Brick concentrates on El Caballo in the on-deck circle, who's looking malignly at Benny Gross floundering on the mound.

El Caballo holds his bat in one hand and swings it windmill style, first to one side and then to the other. He follows that with several cuts before another round of windmills, his eyes never wavering from his feeble target.

The umpire sings out, "Ball three."

Shelly says, "If he walks Oaks, the bases will be loaded for El Caballo, who could put this series away with one swing of his bat."

A wall phone rings near Ryan and her head snaps in its direction.

Benny Gross gets Javy's sign, blows out a few breaths, and throws an outside pitch.

The ump points to first and shouts, "Take your base!"

"And there it is. He walked him," says Dan. "The bases are loaded with no outs!"

Brick calls time and puts down his clipboard before meandering to the mound.

Javy jogs out to meet him.

By the time Brick joins Javy and Benny on the mound, Ryan bursts out of the tunnel and on the field to frenzied cheers.

As Ryan heads toward the mound, flashbacks explode in her mind like gunshots.

She's holding rocks in the pouring rain as Ito holds the stopwatch.

She hits baseballs, righty and lefty, off a swing trainer.

154

Phineas gives her the locket on her thirteenth birthday.

Brick hands Ryan the ball and says, "Sic 'em, kid."

"Crush that cocky bitch," Gil orders El Caballo.

The behemoth first baseman shifts his shuddery eyes to Ryan and lumbers to the plate.

Before jogging away, Javy says, "*Su culo gordo ha estado acaparando el plato toda la noche. Hazle bailar al ritmo de la música de la barbilla,* bruh." (His fat ass has been hogging the plate all night. Make him dance to some chin music, bruh.)

With her fiery eyes fixed on El Caballo, Ryan pulls out her locket, unclasps it to kiss the inside, and is shocked to see a sparkling diamond. Ito had it formed from Phineas' ashes at the facility she'd told him about after the burial. She feels tears rushing to her eyes, but she cuts their flow by sucking in a hard breath. She says, "You're my hero, Ito," before pointing at him and tapping her locket twice.

"It looks like she's pointing to her adoptive father, Ito Hachi," Dan explains.

Ryan kisses the diamond, tucks it into her jersey, and pulls down the bill of her cap.

"She's pulled it down just a little lower than she has all series," says Shelly.

El Caballo stomps his feet into the batter's box one at a time. His dense weight bludgeons the powdery ground, which puffs up around his cleats.

Ryan holds her set for a moment and says, "This is for you, Daddy," before throwing a screaming dart just under the big man's nose.

El Caballo points his bat at Ryan. "You can get away with that 'cause you're a girl."

Ryan flips off her glove and shouts, "Bring it, chunky ass."

Javy belly laughs and chokes out, "Chunky ass. That some funny shit, yo!"

El Caballo points his bat at Javy. "It's not gonna be so funny when I—"

"And words are being exchanged between Javy Diaz and El Caballo," exclaims Dan.

Just before El Caballo and Javy get chest to chest, the home-plate umpire slips between them.

The benches and bullpens empty and spill onto the field, but it simmers down after taunts and threats ping pong between the teams.

With everyone back in place, the umpire slides on his mask and shouts, "Play ball!"

El Caballo spits into his batting gloves, smacks them together, grabs his bat, and glares at Ryan with malice.

Ryan's next pitch pinches the outside corner of the zone. "Steeerike!"

El Caballo looks at the ump and shouts, "C'mon, man. What the hell was that?"

"You arguing balls and strikes? If you think I won't toss you because it's the World Series, just try showing me up again!"

Dan Devine is giddy. "That was a filthy, *filthy* screwball!"

Ryan peers in for the sign, winds up slowly, and tosses a bullet.

El Caballo takes a big hack.

"Two!" shouts the umpire.

Shelly, exhilarated, exclaims, "That fastball was ninety-three. She hasn't hit ninety all year!"

Ryan winds up slowly and tosses a fifty-five MPH drunken knuckleball that staggers in the air, trips, falls, and bounces off the dirt into Javy's glove. The woosh of El

Caballo's swing buckles his back leg and he falls, ungracefully, onto home plate.

Javy whips the ball to Ryan, who spins and throws out Willy on third, who is preoccupied with El Caballo's flop.

Cheers rock the stadium as El Caballo and Stubbs take the walk of shame back to the Waves' dugout.

"Well, look who's back, Shelly."

"Yes, she is, but is she back in time?"

A fan writes "El Caballo" across her tombstone costume and slides it on.

Shelly points. "And the graveyard is forming." She chuckles and says, "I wouldn't be surprised if they made one for Stubbs, too."

Ryan holds the ball on the small of her back and checks Javy for the sign. He calls for a curve ball by dropping a downward peace sign between his legs. Ryan nods, winds up, and spins one.

The batter swings and hits a dribbler that dies halfway between the pitcher's mound and home plate.

Ryan slides, grabs it, knee spins, and throws him out. She pulls her fist down and screams with an open-mouthed wail. The crowd jumps to its feet and roar like charging infantry.

Ito replicates Ryan's fist-pumping scream.

Nelson jumps in the air with a raised fist. "That's my girl! Kick their asses, Ryan!"

"The Hounds need to score six runs in next three innings," says Dan, "and that's if Ryan is perfect."

"And look who's coming to bat," adds Shelly.

Ryan steps into the box to face Robby Carr, a six foot seven, snarky, lefty-handed bean pole with a meaty nose, scaly skin, beady eyes, and stringy black hair that flops around when he pitches. He looks to his catcher, who turns toward Gil Todd, who's tugging his ear lobes, pulling his nose, swiping his hand across his chest, and rubbing the bill of his cap.

The catcher relays the sign, Carr nods, winds up, and hits Ryan with a fastball on the plastic shield covering her elbow.

The umpire points to Carr, indicating a warning, and the benches clear for the second time in the inning.

"That is suspicious, Shelly. Carr has had pinpoint control all night."

Javy bolts from the dugout toward the mound, but Ryan cuts him off. "It isn't worth it, Javy. I need you in the game."

Sando and El Caballo are chest to chest and Benny Gross and Johnny Oaks bark in each other's faces. After more threats and posturing, the players part ways and gorilla-walk back to their own turf.

Ryan and Brick are on the first-base line. "You okay?" asks Brick.

"Absolutely, boss. He throws like a bitch."

Shelly chuckles, "Ryan and Brick share a laugh on her way to first base. She really is a superstar in every possible way."

Ryan draws Robby Carr's attention as she takes a healthy lead off of first.

Carr throws over and Ryan dives back.

Brick shakes his head. "That girl's gonna give me a dang heart attack one day."

Ryan shouts, "You could throw here all night, Robbie, but I'm stealing second base! I am stealing second base!"

"It looks to me like Ryan is taunting Carr," says Dan.

"She is! She's pointing at second base!"

Robbie Carr looks at Ryan several times but as soon as he commits to home, Ryan busts it out like a sprinter after the gunshot.

The catcher stands up for a pitchout and fires to second.

The umpire flings his arms out to his sides and bellows, "Safe!"

"Oh, she's sending a message, all right," exclaims Shelly. "Don't you tell me she's not firing up her teammates right now. Their matriarch is back, bold, and ready to rock and roll!"

Javy walks to the plate and Ryan crouches low on second base with her hands on her knees, looking toward the catcher. She motions to Javy as though she's stealing signs.

The catcher calls time and conferences with Carr on the mound.

Carr, sweating, looks back at Ryan, who challenges him with a monstrous lead. Carr looks home, back at Ryan, back home, and then back to Ryan again before releasing a pitch that Javy flicks to shallow right field.

Willy Stubbs charges the ball and Ryan bolts toward third with no intention of stopping.

Brick is sending signs to stop but Ryan charges with her head down.

Willy catches it on a bounce and fires it to the catcher who blocks Ryan's path ten feet up the baseline. When he bends to glove the ball, Ryan dives over his head, her hands hit home plate in a forward roll, and the fans combust.

An unnerved police officer calls his precinct. "We need backup at Greyhound Stadium. We need all the bodies you can spare, right away. This place is gonna blow!"

"What an astonishing feat of athleticism!" shouts Dan.

The Hounds are high-fiving Ryan and jumping up and

down like Little Leaguers.

Ike Green gets up and bounces one through second and third, scoring Javy, and Abnar Cruz's bomb puts the Hounds right back in the game. It's four-to-five Waves.

Shelly screams, "And here come the Hounds!"

Gil taps his right arm on his way to the mound and takes the ball from Carr, who walks to the dugout, grabs a bat, and thwacks the water cooler with repeated blows as his teammates scatter. When the cooler goes down, he swats at a row of bubble gum containers, which volcano up and cover the floor.

Carr's replacement is removed after getting two outs, but he loads the bases as well.

Gil taps his left arm and Tree Willis breaks out of the pen like a steer in a rodeo.

Dan Devine says, "Gil is bringing in his Hound-killer a little early tonight."

"I don't blame him," says Shelly. "He wants to shut this down, right now."

Tree Willis' energy vents out in quick, fidgety head jerks, twitches, and face swipes until he gets into his windup and harnesses that steam into three straight triple-digit pitches, shutting down Sando and leaving the score 5-4 going into the top half of the eighth inning. Factions of each fan-group face off in the crowd as security rushes in to restore order.

Police cars race toward Greyhound Stadium from all over Los Angeles.

"This crowd is fifty percent Hounds, fifty percent Waves, and one hundred percent rowdy. Man oh man, do I ever love my job." Shelly beams.

Ryan gets back to work and puts down the Waves in order in both the eighth and ninth innings, striking out five of the six batters.

Dan Devine watches Ryan punch the air after throwing her final strike. "And that brings us to the bottom of the ninth in the most memorable game in MLB history."

Shelly adds, "The mission is simple – Tree Willis has to get three men out, and the Hounds have to score a run to tie the game."

"Yes, Shelly. Gil took a chance bringing Tree in early, because if the Hounds tie it, Ryan is fresh, but Tree has been throwing over 100 MPH for a few innings. I predict Willis is going to empty his tank, assuming that this is his last."

Felix Mendoza is the first batter to step into the box.

Tree Willis throws a 102 MPH inside fastball.

Felix swings and pops it up to right field.

Stubbs doesn't even have to move. He catches it with ease and throws it to Tree.

The Hounds fans are wearing their hats backwards and inside out, hoping for a rally.

Felix gets into the dugout and pulls a temper tantrum similar to Robbie Carr's savagery.

Ryan puts on a helmet and pulls her bat out of its slot.

Dan Devine looks at Shelly. "That's one pitch and one out. I'm a little surprised Felix swung at the first one."

"I agree, Dan. If the Hounds tie the score and Tree is still fresh, you can bet your house we'll see him in the tenth."

Tree works fast to speed up the game. As soon as he gets the ball from his catcher, he throws it. His third pitch to Ike Green nearly beans him.

Ike hits the dirt and, when he gets up, he eyes Tree.

Brick shouts, "Stay calm, Ike, he's trying to get in your head. Keep it cool, now."

Tree's next pitch is high, tight, and flicks Ike's uniform.

The umpire gestures a hit batsman and points to first.

Gil comes out and argues, to no avail.

"And there's life yet," says Dan.

Edgar Wright digs in, and after a few foul tips, rips a line drive to El Caballo on first, who catches it and nearly ends the game with a double play, but Ike dives back just in time.

Dan Devine shouts, "Oh my! He was safe by an eyelash!"

Shelly looks at Ryan, holding her bat. "And we all knew it would come down to this. Didn't we? Isn't this the way it always works out? But Brick has a choice to make. He can either take Ryan out and hope for a homer off the bench or—"

"Bunt," Brick says to Ryan. "But you gotta beat it out so's we can pass the baton to Javy.

Ryan nods and walks to the plate.

Dan exclaims, "The last time Tree Willis and Ryan Stone faced each other was in an open tryout and Tree broke Ryan's elbow."

"Oh yeah," Shelly says. "And that might have had something to do with the Willis-Oaks trade. This matchup, right now, will be talked about as the biggest trade of the season. It's Tree Willis verses Ryan Stone, with the World Series hanging in the balance."

Nelson Hernandez is up against the glass in his office.

Tree's first pitch is a 103 MPH inside fastball that backs Ryan off the plate.

The fans scream a hailstorm of jibes and cheers. Their stamping feet rock the playing field.

Tree twitches and blinks before winding up and releasing his pitch.

Ryan lays down a bunt toward third, but it rolls over the baseline.

The umpire screams, "Foul ball!"

Ryan jogs back from first.

When Ryan steps into the box, she sees a vision of Phineas from the last time they spoke on the mansion's ball field.

Phineas says, "You cannot be an adult unless you're able to make a decision and own the result. I still believe in the plan, but it's time for you to decide what's best for you. And it's time for me to leave...

"Good-bye, Ryan."

Ryan looks at him and smiles. "Goodbye, Daddy."

Phineas kisses Ryan, and she walks in the direction of home plate.

Ryan hears her name and she turns back.

"I'm so proud of you, Ryan."

Ryan smiles wide.

Phineas blows her a kiss, then waves at her. He jumps in his Ferrari and drives off.

Ryan goes to the plate and hits the remote button that reawakens the pitching machine.

Ryan is back in the batter's box in the present, looking at Tree Willis jerking and twitching.

Ryan flashes back to the mansion's field as she takes her father's advice and squares to bunt. The pitching machine winds up.

Tree Willis winds up.

The pitching machine fires. Ryan sees the ball coming and changes gears. She pulls the bat back from the bunting position to swing.

Tree's triple-digit pitch shoots toward Ryan. Ryan swings away and the ball explodes off the barrel of her bat.

Johnny Oaks has a bead on it as he confidently moves toward the centerfield wall in the deepest part of the stadium. He leaps, but the ball sails over his glove and lands in the seats.

BORN FOR THE GAME

Dan Devine shouts in falsetto, "She's done it again! Ryan Stone has shocked the baseball world! The Hounds win the World Series! The Hounds win the World Series!"

Ito jumps up and down like a child.

By the time Ryan rounds second base, fans have blown by the bolstered police barricade and lined up on both sides of the baselines, giving her a hero's pathway to home plate, where her teammates are gathered.

Rollie jumps up and down in his living room, cheering. He shouts, "Secrecy, MLB by nineteen. Best ever! Best ever! Best ever!"

Quin loads suitcases in his trunk, gets in his car, drives up the street and disappears into the night.

Shelly looks down at the field. "It is absolute pandemonium down there as the police are dragging fans away. Fortunately, many are jumping back into the stands."

The Hounds move as one toward the dugout as Gil Todd, Tree Willis, Johnny Oaks, Willy Stubbs, El Caballo, and the rest of the Waves look on.

Ryan hugs Brick and gives him a hard kiss on the cheek.

Brick says, "C'mon, Ryan, cut that out or I'm gonna have to fine you five thousand dollars!" He laughs. "As long as you play for me, I will never doubt you again."

The screaming, exuberant team charges into the locker room wearing World Champion T-shirts and hats. Some of the players are recording it on their cells. The room is sectioned off with shower curtains for their long-awaited Champagne celebration.

The press snaps pictures and broadcasts the event.

Champagne showers erupt like hot springs as the players run around soaking each other.

Javy and Abnar comfort Sando, who is crying in a corner.

Nelson sneaks up behind Brick and pours Champagne down the back of his pants.

"You son of a bitch! I'm-a fine you, too, Nellie!"

Victory evokes the stories of all their lives, which play out around the room, some in private, others spoken into a reporter's microphone.

Sando holds a microphone with a firm grip and shouts, "This is for you, Vincent!"

After the celebration subsides, the room faces Dan Devine and Shelly Shaw, who stand with Nelson Hernandez, Brick Jackson, and the Commissioner of Baseball, Sherman Tucker.

Tucker smiles wide, holding a large trophy.

Ito looks on from just off camera, to the right of the Hounds' brass.

Dan Devine shouts, "Let's get Ryan Stone up here."

Ryan's teammates shoot Champagne at her as she walks up to the mic.

Shelly says, "At this time, I'd like to introduce the commissioner of Major League Baseball, Sherman Tucker."

Tucker takes the microphone. "Thanks so much, Shelly." He looks at Ryan. "It is my great honor and privilege to name Ryan Stone as the World Series MVP." He hands the trophy to Ryan, who looks at it with a tight-lipped smile in an attempt to buffer up the dam behind her eyes. After a few moments, she finds her voice.

"Thank you so much, Mr. Tucker. I would like to thank my teammates..." The guys cheer, which causes Ryan to pause for a moment. "Yes, my teammates... with a special thanks to Javy Diaz, Nelson Hernandez, and Brick Jackson."

More cheers.

Ryan sniffles and takes a moment to collect herself before speaking again. "Most of all, I'd like to say that I've been blessed with a happy home, love, and a beautiful vision from my dad, Phineas Stone, of whom I am very proud... and for my father, Ito Hachi, without whom I wouldn't be here today. I dedicate this trophy to both of them."

Cheers ring out from the crowd, but they are quelled by a woman's voice.

"And what about your mother?"

Ryan turns to see Valentina Fermi standing beside Ito. Ryan runs to Valentina and engulfs her. Flashes pop as the media surrounds them.

Valentina looks at Ryan up close through blurry eyes and kisses her on both cheeks repeatedly. With her cheek against Ryan's, Valentina says, "I'm going to take you to Italy so you can meet all of your family. Ito too, because he's family."

Ryan wipes her tears away. "Yes, he is... Mom?"

Valentina says, "I've waited twenty years to hear that!"

Ryan sees Ito looking vulnerable for the first time in her life, and she goes to him and puts her hands on his shoulders. "Thank you for everything, Ito." Ryan and Ito look at each other for a beat and she hugs him, tightly, rocking back and forth, squeezing tears from the corners of his eyes.

Ryan puts her arms around Valentina and Ito, which turns the room into a strobe as camera flashes pop in rapid succession. This pose transitions into a newspaper headline reading:

RYAN STONE
Simply The Best

Being Brothers takes place in the Bronx in 1973. It's the time of street games, riding bikes without helmets, drinking from hoses, and the wonderful world before cell phones. It explores family, friendship, and the profound impact of our past. It's available on Amazon as a paperback, audiobook, and eBook.

"This book is as refreshing for the kids of the 1970's, as Grease was for the kids of the fifties."

"It (Being Brothers) was by far my best Christmas gift and my daughter is finishing it as I write this, probably with a lump in her throat and a few tears in her eyes. I urge you to read this book as soon as you can!"

"Through Mike DeLucia's descriptiveness, I felt as though I was once again eleven years old back in the Bronx. What a joy it was to reconnect with cherished childhood memories."

Who's the greatest basketball player ever?

Madness is the intriguing story of Hank Luisetti, the predawn of March Madness, and how modern basketball was born.

"So many compelling reasons to keep passing this book of Mike DeLucia's around..."

"The bottom line is that Madness is pound for pound the best basketball book I have read in many, many years and I urge you to give it a read."

"I am so impressed by this writer's ability to convey a story of overcoming obstacles and standing up for what you believe."

"A riveting account of a basketball unknown who changes the game. The author was like an announcer at a game making the game exciting and the story interesting."

"DeLucia's storytelling is as energetic as being courtside at one of Luisetti's games."

Acknowledgements

Thank you!

Lucia Chiarelli
Lillian DeLucia
Cheryl Demaree
Christian DiPeri
John Doherty
Nick Garzillo
William Lobb
Ron MacFarland
Jess Macualay
Deborah Mercora
Sean Piacente
Lou Santos
Anna Savino
Judy Savino
Janice Spina
Laura Wilkinson

Mike De Lucia grew up in the Bronx and has spent most of his life as an entrepreneur, actor, teacher, director, and writer. He is a multi-award-winning author of several books, including the historical fiction novel, *Madness, The Man Who Changed Basketball* and *Being Brothers* the story of two brothers growing up in the Bronx in the early 1970s.

Mike, a green tea enthusiast, travels the world with his wife Lillian, has two children, two grandchildren, and loves receiving emails from readers.

If you enjoy his books, have questions, or are interested in a book talk, please reach out: **greentbooks@gmail.com**

www.booksbymikedelucia.com

Made in United States
North Haven, CT
06 December 2021

12080315R00098